A SIMPLE

LIFE

Snatch in Time

By
Philip Corridan

CONTENTS

AUTHOR'S NOTE

This is a work of fiction. It is set during two summers, the first in East Anglia and the Netherlands in 2019, the second in Greece in 2039. Places briefly mentioned are given their real name but much of the action takes place in 'the village' or 'the city'. These are not named because they don't exist as described - I have taken liberties with both geography and time. Norfolk has a number of broads and dykes, and certainly plenty of marinas but Eastland Broad, Davison's Dyke and the Mermaid Cove Marina don't exist either, they are purely fictional. The Greek settings are real, and I've given the place names English speakers normally use, although Greek to English name translation is not always straightforward.

Much of the book has been written on board a boat but you don't have to be a boating person to read it ...

PROLOGUE

Please join me viewing some footage taken by a drone. There's no soundtrack so it's just eye and brain as we approach Great Yarmouth from the sea. The drone is high enough to see the river Yare on its two-mile passage through the town harbour before it joins (or leaves) the North Sea.

Norfolk, Nelson's County said that road sign as you drove here. We pass over the tall column known as the Britannia Monument, dedicated to Nelson, before turning north then west once more to fly over the river as it expands to become Breydon Water. Narrowing again at Breydon's end, a branch of the river heads south, becoming the Waveney. We head south-west with the Yare as it flows through grazing marshes. It's a fine early summer day and we are high enough to see many miles inland. Norfolk is a flat county (or has 'big skies' in tourist brochure language) so soon we'll be able to see the city at the end of the navigable river. Before that though, try half closing your eyes to emphasise the scene's main colours. A silver thread snaking through green at its sides and blue above. All pale shades, a restful combination, colours seen looking up through a silver birch tree to the sunny sky perhaps.

The drone flies lower as we near Reedham where a yacht is tacking up towards the swing bridge. She'll have to wait, trains have priority and there's one approaching slowly, ready to cross the river on its way to Lowestoft. You notice a pub, the Lord Nelson. Yes, it's one of a number in this county proud to be the birthplace of one of England's greatest heroes. As we continue, just north of west now, river traffic increases, mostly motorboats but the occasional sailing craft too. We pass a sugar beet factory on the north side of the river, sited here a long time ago when local sailing craft (Norfolk Wherries) delivered sugar beet straight from fields bordering the river. The last delivery by wherry was in the late 1950s. It's all done by lorries thundering along country roads these days.

Here's another pub on the south bank, the Beauchamp Arms. You say the pub's name as if in France. Ah no, you're in Norfolk now, round here we say Beechum Arms. And there are plenty of other examples of simplification of local place names - Happisburgh (Hazebruh), Wymondham (Windum), Stiffkey (Stooki) and, just when you think you've got a grip on this subject, you come across Haddiscoe, confidently pronounce it something like Hadsco only to find that it's said locally just as it looks. You can't win. As they say, in Norfolk we *do diffrent.*

Soon we reach a village which is clearly a major boating centre. The drone hovers at the entrance to a large marina at the eastern end of the village.

MERMAID COVE MARINA
PRIVATE MOORINGS
NO HIREBOATS

states the huge signboard. It doesn't ban drones though so in we sneak. Here reside luxury motorboats, or motor yachts as sales brochures put it, or gin palaces as those who don't have one tend to call them. Let's settle on calling them motor yachts, it suits their gleaming white fibreglass and stainless steel, their general statement of power and the good life. These motor yachts tie securely to floating pontoons designed to cope with the range of tidal movement. Plugged into mains electricity to keep the battery banks up, they make perfect weekend cottages. There's no doubt that the Mermaid Cove is a 5-star full-service marina providing all that the wealthy boat owner needs. Or what the once-wealthy-until-buying-a-boat person needs. Or perhaps doesn't need but is paying for anyway. That's the thing with this sort of marina, it's as much a display of wealth as boating skill.

Affluence tends to pall if you don't have it, so the drone moves silently on past smaller boatyards and a riverside shop, the Ferry Stores, until at the west end of the village we notice a narrow tree lined cut off the river. Davison's Dyke says a small and grubby sign. From here old Mr Davison ran his motor cruiser hireboat business in the 1930s - your grandparents may remember framed advertisements in ancient railway carriages urging travellers to

HOLIDAY AFLOAT ON THE NORFOLK BROADS!

And most of the Davison customers did arrive by train, lugging on foot their suitcases the half mile from the station. Their expectation? A freedom to explore a watery world for seven or fourteen days, living a life far removed from their usual one.

Today's more worldly-wise hirers expect secure parking for their cars and their hired boats to be equipped with Wi-Fi, satellite TV/DVD, fridge freezers and bathroom with shower as a minimum. They won't be on a holiday afloat on the Norfolk Broads of course, instead they have been encouraged to

DISCOVER BRITAIN'S MAGICAL WATERLAND

We'll never find out what old Mr Davison thinks of the current state of play, both he and his sons are long gone now, and their wooden hire fleet rotted away many years ago. Two things haven't changed though, it's still a narrow dyke with room for moored boats on one side only, and these moorings are still just the natural dyke bank. No electricity, no water tap, no nice quay with mooring posts, just raw bank as the Davison family knew it. The drone seems unwilling to move on from this spot which provides a balance to the conspicuous consumption of the Mermaid Cove Marina. Here 24 smaller, older and certainly more worn boats tie mostly to bits of old scaffold pole hammered haphazardly into the dyke bank leaving four or five feet above ground to stop boats floating onto the path when the dyke floods its banks, an increasingly frequent event. A well-known joke has it that things happen in Norfolk somewhat later than in other parts of the UK, but global warming doesn't get this joke and flooding proceeds here at the same quickening pace as elsewhere.

At the Mermaid Cove you park your merc, jag or beamer by your boat but owners of boats at Davison's Dyke have to park their vehicle at the top of a steep lane off the main village road, walk down this lane, over a railway line and across a field to reach an unlocked gate. From here there's a rough footpath between the trees and the boats. The dyke, the stand of trees each side and the nearby marshy fields are privately owned these days, by an Arab they say, but whoever owns the property has a land agent to whom the 24 boat owners pay their fees. At £7.50 per foot of boat length per quarter these are the cheapest moorings in the village.

Just one of the dyke's collection of boats is a sailing vessel - Sandpiper, a scruffy 26-foot-long plywood yacht of the Eventide class bought cheaply by Paul Williams a couple of years ago. Cheap yes, but it cost pretty much all he had plus £500 borrowed from his mother. Paul's not assertive and, sadly for him, he chose a solicitor to match so has not done well out of the divorce settlement. He continues to pay the mortgage for the ex-matrimonial home where his former wife lives with Ben, their four-year-old son. He also pays maintenance for Ben and as a result lives a hand to mouth existence on his boat here at the dyke, just half a mile from his son's home. Hand to mouth wouldn't be Paul's description though. He says he lives a simple life, getting by with a battery powered radio, a gas heater and a two-ring gas cooker. A small solar panel just about keeps up with demand on the boat's battery. For water, gas and food he rows Sandpiper's battered tender downriver to Ferry Stores, a twice a week 20-minute exercise he usually enjoys. On land Paul gets about on an elderly bike to which he's added a child's seat. As he says, it's a simple life and he's happy that he's achieving his main aim of providing Ben with as loving and stress free a childhood as possible in the circumstances.

Is he happy in himself you ask? Perhaps, for the time being, it's hard to tell, we'll see, who knows ... only vague answers seem appropriate at the moment.

It's 11 p.m. on a May evening and the only boat with a light on is Sandpiper ...

ONE

2019

Paul glanced at the clock. With a 9 a.m. class to teach in the morning he should be asleep by now. Instead, he switched off the cabin light and waited for his eyes to adjust to the darkness before opening the hatch to be in the warm evening for a final minute or two. He felt a sense of peace, a rightness in the world. In the dark around him and in the water below, night creatures lived and died he supposed, but they did so unseen and in silence. Looking skyward he had the impression that clouds filled most of what could be seen. Looking down the dyke towards the river he could just make out the shape of neighbouring boats floating obediently on their moorings, their scuffed appearance in daylight becoming almost romantic and mysterious in darkened outline. Looking up the dyke it was just black until, in the direction of the gate, he saw a glow briefly intensify red then dim. Will 'O the Wisp, that old East Anglian myth?

'Don't be stupid,' he muttered to himself then suddenly thought - cigarette? Was someone standing smoking at the gate? And watching him?

Another glow, then some seconds later another from the same place. Definitely someone smoking. He was being watched. But who would want to do that? A fellow mooring holder would surely shout hello or come over. Or were thieves waiting for the only liveaboard on the dyke to retire for the night? No, not thieves, they would come by water, by road it's too far to lug stolen items to where a van would have to park. And the dyke doesn't have the sort of boats from which there's much to steal.

No matter how hard he looked there was nothing to see against the dense trees apart from this occasional glow. At 35, six foot two and reasonably fit, the sort of fitness that comes from cycling 10 miles to and from college, he knew most people would expect him to put on shoes and investigate. But with no experience of physical confrontation since early school days he found it only too easy to wait and see.

Trying to breathe slowly and easily, he continued to look in the direction of the gate until convinced that the watcher had gone. Or stopped smoking, perhaps when the watcher found himself watched in return. Still Paul waited and it was after midnight when he laid his bike along the gangplank between the boat and the path as a sort of stumble-with-associated-noise alarm. You're being foolish and melodramatic he thought but this didn't stop him taking a hammer from the toolbox and placing it within reach of his berth. Sliding the hatch closed, he undressed and, avoiding the usual knock-out pill, wriggled into the sleeping bag after a last check through the starboard window. On his back he lay finding it impossible to relax the body while the mind listened for sounds of an intruder.

Gunton. There seemed no time interval between not knowing then thinking he knew who the watcher was. Paul remembered that the man had a smirk on his face when they'd crossed paths and nodded to each other outside the village chandlers a couple of days ago. Gunton was perhaps an inch shorter than him but heavier built and broader in the shoulder. This bruiser's body topped by a head with close cropped hair and bull neck combined to give Gunton an air of menace, heightened by his habit of standing only a few inches away when talking face to face. About half the distance normal people keep, making him an unwelcome space invader. Not that Paul had personal experience of this, but he'd seen him talking to others. In short, Gunton was the sort of man he felt uncomfortable with and usually avoided.

The alarm woke him at 7 a.m. and it was a few seconds before he remembered last night, then felt ashamed that he'd slept soundly. He slid open the hatch and peered out. Things seemed normal and he was relieved to find that the bike alarm remained where he'd left it. Then he noticed that the footpath was flooded once more. It would be another day of wearing wellingtons for now and slipping shoes into his briefcase to put on at college.

He smiled, partly in relief that last night's episode seemed to be of no consequence and partly at the memory of the course leader, Geoff Nutt, saying, 'You're teaching management maths to accountants, not pig rearing to farmers,' following complaints from students insulted by the appearance of their welly clad lecturer, so different from his suited colleagues. 'The students find your apparently casual approach disconcerting,' the course leader had continued, 'and inappropriate in that your subject is thought to be one of the toughest of their professional exams.' Paul had promised to try harder to look the part and had even gone as far as putting washed shirts on hangers to dry making them look vaguely like ironed ones from a distance, or not as creased as before perhaps.

8 a.m. Locking the hatch and adding shoes to the lecture notes and sandwich in his briefcase, Paul strapped it onto the child seat, not needed for its primary purpose until access day tomorrow. He wheeled the bike onto a footpath covered by ankle deep water and waded through the gate and across the field. The ground was dry by the time he reached the railway line, so it was quicker progress up the lane

until he was finally able to pedal away on the back road to college.

He should be concentrating on safe cycling of course but three miles of country road and two of city often provided the opportunity to rehearse the morning's topic - in his second year of teaching he was rarely more than a few minutes ahead of the students. For the last few days though he'd been distracted by a sort-of-rhythmic sort-of-verse brought on by seeing what may once have been a blackbird, body flattened on the road yet with its wings oddly pointing to the sky.

Wings sprout from the road
A tribute to their owner, now flat
Once they flew through the air
Now it flows past them
Vapour from the immaculate killing machine
Man made, obscene
Dull sheen on my lungs
Lead in my head
Forcing my extremes
When I could live in between

He supposed his Eng Lit colleagues would find it laughable (and leaded petrol had long gone of course) but the poem/verse or whatever it was fitted his cycling rhythm ... man made, obscene, dull sheen ...

He recalled reading somewhere that the young Wilfred Owen in his first job as an assistant to a vicar would cycle to visit parishioners, composing and evaluating lines as he pedalled. What the Eng Lits would make of this link with the esteemed WW1 poet didn't bear thinking about. Sod 'em. That no one knew about this side of him added to his pleasure.

Paul had been teaching Maths and Stats to the Accountancy Foundation class for eight months. Their exams were only three weeks away and he'd been revising the major topics on which they would be examined. Towards the end of last week, he'd given each of them a photocopied couple of pages from Robert Persig's book Zen and the Art of Motorcycle Maintenance. He didn't have the permission of the copyright owner but the book had been published 40 or 50 years earlier so he didn't think there would be a problem.

This afternoon's session was the last of the day for both himself and the class. He'd felt an air of simmering resentment as soon as he entered the room. Assuming that their preceding class had gone badly, he tried to jolly them along, get some response. In vain, a sullen silence prevailed for almost the whole length of the session leading him to use up at least two weeks' worth of teaching material. Finally coming to the Persig photocopy he mentioned the structure of significance testing.

'Of what use is motorcycle maintenance to us, or Zen for that matter?' said Briony Barton-Jones. It was said as an icy statement of contempt rather than a question. Briony, delicious, gorgeous nineteen-year-old Briony, the English rose for whom pedestals were invented. Her statement made with all the certainty her privileged middle-class upbringing guaranteed. She was not alone, heads nodded, and he heard a few mutterings of 'yes' as she finished.

'I used this excerpt because you all know what a motorcycle looks like and the author uses plain language to describe a procedure that I thought you would find akin to significance testing.'

He'd barely finished before most of the class seemed to be speaking, one or two to him but mostly to each other. He caught snatches of conversations ...

'that's utter nonsense'
'wellington boots'
'he also gave us that reading from a novel where some idiot had calculated a correlation coefficient to ten decimal places'
'and exams in three weeks'
'Zen and the art of balance sheets'

He'd had no previous experience of this, this what ... class disintegration? He stood helpless. Talking continued, a few faces (the expected ones) seem to be laughing at him, at his lack of control. Enjoying some sort of revenge? In the midst of this he saw Adebola, that always smiling, clever Nigerian in the front row tear off a sheet from his pad, write on it and push it towards him. 'Are you associated with a School of Mystic?' Adebola's note asked, adding to Paul's sense of dislocation.

Looking up from Adebola's note he shook his head in answer then noticed that Emma at the right-hand end of the third row of desks was speaking to him. 'I thought it was an interesting and useful excerpt.' He half heard; half lip read her words.

'Thank you,' he mouthed back to her. Emma, 32, married, the only mature student in the class was showing support. Given how heavily outnumbered she was her action was more than kind.

But it didn't stop the chaos. Another person might have shouted authoritatively for order but Paul's desire to escape had become overwhelming. It was only ten minutes to the official class ending time so he put his papers in his briefcase and made for the door with as much dignity as he could muster. Which became very little as he heard someone say, 'running away now.'

Nearing the door, he saw Emma's left hand stretch out low into the aisle. He took this to be an unobtrusive display of sympathy that no one else probably noticed. He let his left hand briefly touch her arm as he passed and then he was gone from the room. In auto he must have gone back to the staff room, stowed today's notes and readied tomorrow's though the next action he could later remember was one of unlocking the staff cycle shed.

Too tired to pedal the five miles back to the village he put the bike on the train and sat opposite it, suddenly sniggering as he thought of a variation on an old Music Hall joke. 'Class with me all the way.' 'Managed to shake them off at the station.'

And School of Mystic, what was it about himself that had prompted the question? The word Zen? Was he so far from the norm?

A few minutes later, sun providing a strobe effect on his closed eyelids as the train moved along its tree-lined track, he thought of Briony. Such a gloriously attractive female, such a waspish sting, he wondered how many men she would slaughter in her lifetime. Ah, beautiful, beautiful Briony, who will be the first to chew your knickers off, he wondered. For all he knew first could be a past event and she was already enjoying off-chewings, probably not though. But if first is still in the future then the one certainty is that the event won't feature Paul Williams, the contempt in her voice had been unmistakeable. And here he was on the train, the welly clad clod attempting to claw back some parity by coarseness. Williams the Unworthy. Then he wondered how long he would survive as a teacher. The eight-week summer break was only six weeks away, surely he'll last until then? He'd been preparing Sandpiper for a possible cruise to Holland, buying bargain boat bits as and when he could afford them. He comforted himself with the realisation that he'd just catch the village chandlery before they shut for the day.

He closed the chandler's door and turned, almost bumping straight into a man in bomber jacket and jeans. Gunton took half a step forward to be a few inches away. 'Bin keeping an eye on you,' he said.

An estuarian accent. Paul fought to avoid appearing as disconcerted as he felt, the bloody man was standing so close. Gunton's round face and large, almost feminine eyes seemed at odds with the brawler's nose and the rest of his menacing appearance. And staring directly at me, no head movement, no mannerisms, disconcerting is not a strong enough word, Paul thought. He knew that he had to avoid seeming weak by asking why he was being watched. 'You were smoking at the gate last night, about 11 p.m.,' he eventually replied.

Gunton didn't bother to acknowledge it. 'We've something you'll be interested in; we need to talk.'

Thinking this meant a boat bit they thought they

could sell him, Paul held up the small galvanised shackle he'd just bought. 'I don't think so, this is my level of buying power.'

'That's why you want to hear what we can do for you. I'll be in the White Hart at eight tomorrow.' Gunton's eyes didn't leave Paul's until the last second as the man walked past, missing his shoulder by less than half an inch. Somehow this was more threatening than an actual shoulder barge and Paul stayed still for a few seconds to calm his nerves. A little taller, probably fitter and 15 years or so younger he shouldn't be afraid of the man but, in his current state of mental fragility, all he wanted to do was get back to the boat and leave a world that seemed to have quickly changed into a confrontational one.

Looking both ways before pushing the bike across the road his eyes lingered on Gunton as he walked away, taking short steps. He knew these often mean relatively short legs and large upper body. He'd read somewhere that upper body strength was a characteristic of many professionals in contact sports, retired footballers Paul Gascoigne and Michael Laudrup being prime examples. And boxers? He'd heard Gunton had been one in his youth and still worked occasionally as a nightclub bouncer. A man to avoid he thought, yet again, then remembered he'd just been invited (it seemed something stronger) to meet tomorrow. And the man had used the plural, 'what *we* can do for you' ... what was going on?

Sitting in the cabin later that evening he revisited the afternoon's disastrous class. Less than twenty-four hours ago a relaxed, contented man slid open the hatch to enjoy a last few minutes in the warmth of the evening. Look at him now, destroyed by Briony, disturbed by Gunton. The afternoon disaster of a class was made worse by knowing it was an own goal. The mistake was his, he should not have been trying some broad brush or perspective approach this close to their exams. He should just have done what the other teachers did and work through answers to old exam papers. Course entry required A levels so the students could have gone to university first to get a more rounded education before studying accountancy. In contrast, the students in his class had chosen to become qualified accountants as soon as possible. How had he lost sight of this? Too bound up with his own situation? Convinced he knows best?

Should he be teaching at all? In the past he'd worked as an engineer, an office kind of one where he could get away with playing the slightly strange backroom techie role. There was no doubt that he was more suited to this than to teach students to pass examinations, which is pretty much the only type of course his college offered. The reason he completed a teacher's certificate at all was that if his ex-wife and son moved to another part of the country then he'd be able to follow and have a reasonable chance of finding a nearby teaching post. Not an honourable reason for taking up teaching, he knew, but his son Ben came first. Needs must. And thinking of must, he had to find a way of thanking Emma face to face. That afternoon she had displayed sympathy for a fellow human in distress. His one positive for the day.

News of his classroom failure would be widely known by tomorrow evening. Tomorrow was also access day and Paul had two easy-to-deal-with classes in the morning then he'd be free to pick up Ben after lunch. He resolved to get into college ten minutes early in the morning and try to see the course leader. He'd be contrite, promise to focus on exam preparation from now on, accept a bollocking. There seemed no other option if he wanted to continue teaching.

Arriving in college early the following day Paul found that his plan of last night had been pre-empted. An envelope sat centrally on his desk. Addressed to Mr P E Williams in the department secretary's handwriting. Inside he found himself continuing to be addressed formally, a bad sign. The only sentence in the memo informed him that he had an appointment with the principal lecturer in accountancy at 0900 tomorrow. He realised there must have been a deputation from the class to the principal lecturer yesterday afternoon.

Christ, everyone must know by now. He could feel his face going red. What a fool, he should have gone straight to the course leader after escaping from the class. Though that would not have done much good as the deputation had gone straight to the next level up. He supposed this said something uncomplimentary about the difference between his sense of entitlement and theirs.

Other teachers sharing the staffroom started to arrive, their immediate uneasiness making it clear that the grapevine had worked with its usual efficiency. Who in their right mind wanted to be associated with failure or ineptitude? Paul could get away with being the department oddball only if others accept him as competent, a standing he'd just lost. At this point a C grade film script might have a more experienced teacher say a few kind words, an arm around the shoulder perhaps. Or that hitherto reserved lady on the other side of the room make a point of coming over to speak. This was reality though, and awkwardness prevailed until Paul left for his first class.

The morning passed uneventfully as he concentrated on his teaching. Walking back to the staff room he found Emma waiting to catch him, looking apprehensive. He approached her smiling. 'Thank you so much for the show of support yesterday. It was truly appreciated,' he said.

'I'm sorry it was necessary. Do you know that

there was a deputation to the principal lecturer right after the class finished?' Despite the content of her message, her voice was surprisingly soft and gentle with a slight East Anglian accent that he hadn't noticed before. In response to his nodded reply she continued. 'I tried to say that they were overreacting, but I couldn't stop them. I don't want to say who they were, but I think that it was five of them who went to see the principal lecturer in the end.'

This close he noticed her brown eyes and her nose with its few freckles. An open, homely and attractive face. 'I can guess who they were. I am summoned to appear before him at nine tomorrow morning but don't worry for me, I'll deal with whatever is the outcome,' he touched her left forearm lightly, 'and once more, thank you for yesterday. Seeing your arm gesture as I walked out stopped me from feeling completely alienated.' 'It made a significant difference,' he added jokingly.

She smiled in return and put her right hand across her body onto his, the one touching her forearm. An awkward yet intimate gesture. I hope no one walks by, he thought, but took no action. She said, 'Thank you. Actually, I've been trying to find an opportunity to speak to you. There are one or two ideas I'd like to discuss. Can we meet over a coffee, say at the Costa on Union Street?'

Her right hand was not heavy on his, but the

pressure was sufficient to maintain their contact and for him to think that her one or two ideas may have little to do with his teaching subject. Maybe he was wrong though, this was a mature married woman, it could all be quite innocent. 'OK, though not now, I have a four-year-old son and today is my afternoon with him. We could have a quick chat after Monday's class and make arrangements.'

'That's good, and I'll have my fingers crossed for you at 9 a.m. tomorrow. And see how you look in class later that morning.' She let go of his hand, allowing him to disengage from her forearm. These were unpractised movements he felt, yet there seemed some sort of rapport or understanding between them that he was still thinking about as he cycled back to the village. Given their touching it was lucky that no member of staff (or, perhaps worse) one of her classmates passed by at the time.

Eventually he forced himself to focus on the highlight of the week, the four hours or so he'd spend on Sandpiper that afternoon with Ben.

TWO

2019

Looking contented Ben sat at the cabin table drawing. It was usually a boating scene, or a four-year-old's view of a boating scene where a smiling stickperson stands on a boat floating on a squiggle of water. Or was it something more? Is he drawing a boating scene because he likes it here, wants to be part of it? If it is Paul thought, then I'm doing something right.

'Daddy, what is water shape?' Ben asked, blue pencil in hand. In the galley his father stopped opening a tin of chilli con carne, Ben usually just drew a wavy line. Putting down the half-opened tin Paul turned, smiled and motioned a wavy line. His son looked at him then twisted around and stared out of the window, making it clear that he knew the water in the dyke was flat. Surprised and then pleased he realised that his son was beyond a simple explanation of the shape of water. But at four years old? What did that high forehead and tangle of black hair hide?

Paul remembered access day last week when rain had bucketed down for 15 minutes. A vertical sea would have been a better description and they had taken shelter in the railway station. A few minutes after the rain had stopped, he was pushing the bike up a hill. In the gutter water rushed past them before falling down a drain. A stone sat on the grid of the drain, too large to fall through. From his seat on the back of the bike, Ben had said. 'Stone not go down, Daddy.'

'The stone is heavier than water,' he'd replied. An accurate statement of course, but not an answer to his son's unasked question. He'd got away with a cop out then, but he wouldn't be able to now. There's no avoiding some sort of molecular explanation he realised. No, surely not that - he quickly reviewed things again. No, there was no other way, molecules it had to be.

Sitting opposite Ben he said, 'Drawing water is hard to do.' Ben nodded, he'd recently discovered the non-verbal yes and no. At his current rate of progress, he'd master a Gallic shrug of indifference by the end of next week.

Paul continued. 'Everything. Everything,' he said again for emphasis, 'is made up of tiny, tiny things called molecules. They are far too small for us to see and there are many different molecules, some much stronger than others.'

He could see the boy's amusement as he silently mouthed the word. A funny, comical sort of word.

'Molecule,' Paul said again, smiling encouragement.

'Molecule,' Ben said finally, not a bad attempt for a four-year-old. Was he going to say this funny word to others in his pre-school group tomorrow? Possibly not, his ex-wife has already been told that Ben tended to play on his own when there. Autism had become fashionable to diagnose only in the last couple of decades. When Paul was a child he was regarded as somewhere on the unsociable scale. A bit of an obsessive. A nerd in today's language. Is his son also showing the signs? Does playing on his own mean that he has already learned that it's not a good idea to appear different?

Having introduced the comical word Paul knew he had to continue. 'Well, molecules join to each other, sort of stick to each other, though we usually use the word bond. Molecules bond to each other.' Paul's hands pretended to stick to each other to demonstrate this last bit.

He got up, filled a bowl with water and brought it back to the table. 'Water has a simple molecule and it does not have a strong bond,' he said, putting his fingers into the water. 'Look, it's easy to push my fingers through it.'

Drying his hands on his jumper he then showed Ben that he could not push his fingers through the cabin table. 'Wood is made up of much bigger molecules than water, and they bond strongly to each other,' Paul said then continued, 'do you remember last week when I was pushing the bike up the hill in the city, after that heavy rain?'

Ben nodded so his father continued. 'Well, water with its simple molecule just slides apart at the metal grid of the drain and falls down through.' He used his fingers once more to demonstrate.

A successful teacher soon learns to recognise the danger of a big hole a second or two before arriving at the point where he or she falls into it. If he isn't careful Paul suddenly realised then he'd have to try to explain about gravity, and that's a very big topic. He'd need a fair bit of preparation before attempting that. Captain Sensible would not have got anywhere near where Paul was at this moment.

Ben was still looking at his father, thinking about water sliding around the drain grid and down perhaps. Please don't ask why it goes *down* Paul silently pleaded. He was in luck, a smile opened on his son's face. 'Strong bond stone,' the boy said.

'Yes, yes!' exclaimed Paul, he'd got through! 'Exactly right,' he leaned forward and ruffled his son's hair. The boy beamed, those lovely gappy infant teeth.

Shape still had to be dealt with though. The water in the bowl had a flat surface again so Paul put his head down and blew gently across the bowl, making small ripples. 'Water's shape depends on the wind. If there is none then the water is flat, like outside the window. But if there is wind then there will be waves.'

Ben nodded once more. He picked up the blue pencil he drew gigantic waves, some higher than the boat. 'Windy,' he said.

The stick man aboard the boat had his arms spread. 'In those waves I think your man will have to hold on tightly,' said Paul.

Ben drew a third arm between the man and boat. 'Three arms are very useful on a boat in bad weather,' said his father, causing Ben to reach for a clean sheet of paper. Those with Autistic or Aspergery tendencies like things to be right. Stickmen should have two arms. Clearly Ben was going to draw the scene again.

It was time to continue with tea. Paul measured out enough rice for one and a half persons, 105 on the jug's ml scale to be followed by 210 ml of water. He wasn't what you'd call a natural cook so did things by numbers. Rice on to boil he finished opening the tin of chilli con carne, put that in a pan on the cooker's only other burner then added a tin of peas. He'd produced the same meal for Ben last week, and for some weeks before. He didn't do variety. He was a vegetarian when his son wasn't there. Hardly a proper vegetarian then, he supposed, but it didn't matter. Ben ate meat or fish at home so he would have the same here, that mattered much more than vegetarian 'purity'. As the pan contents simmered Paul mulled over the last few minutes. The Shape of Water wasn't a new theme. He remembered reading, years ago now, Andrea Camilleri's Montalbano novel of that name, and there was a recent film with that title - he hadn't seen it but knew that the film was another variation on the theme rather than one with a script based on the Camilleri book.

It usually didn't take long before he wallowed in self-criticism. Was his explanation adequate? There were so many aspects he didn't touch on. Sometime soon he'll be forced to explain the nature of air and water, the two mediums we and the things we make move through. And have to breathe and drink, nothing important then! Walking along the street we don't compress air, it just slides around us, reforming itself immediately behind. No vacuum is formed behind items subject to moving air - window cleaners working on skyscrapers, high up on their hoisted platforms, don't run out of air to breathe just because they are working on the lee side of the building. No, air deflects around things and reforms immediately behind, as simple as that. Water behaves similarly and, unlike air, you can see it doing so. He should take Ben to Great Yarmouth soon. They could stand on Haven Bridge and watch the water part and reform around the elderly bridge's thick stone pillars. He smiled. 'Strong bond stone.' That's my boy!

Meal over. Access Day almost over. They packed things away in Ben's box, a large plastic crate occupying most of the space under the starboard cabin berth. There were a few books and a car or two but most of the crate contained flattened cereal packets, egg boxes, match boxes, cotton reels, elastic bands, glue, scissors and the such. Makings, as he and Ben call them. Stuff for the mini engineer to exercise his creative mind on. Stuff with which to bond (ah, bond) with his father.

At Ben's home there was an MGB classic roadster in the drive. It had been there before. Paul rang the bell.

Debbie, his ex-wife, opened the door. Ben rushed past her into the house. A second or two later Paul heard a male voice say. 'Hello Ben.' A deep masculine voice, unlike his own rather high pitched one. After the euphoria of the day Paul's fall was all the harder. As with tides, the highest highs accord with the lowest lows. It was a cliché he knew but there really was a knot in his stomach, and something acidic had replaced his blood.

'We need to talk,' Debbie said.

'About Mr MGB?' he asked, sourly.

'Mr MGB as you call him is just a friend. You and I are divorced you know.'

She stared at him. Debbie had a long face with sharp features that he'd fallen for ten years ago. Now he noticed faint lines stretching from her eyes. Perhaps she's seeing similar signs in me, he thought.

'We need to talk about Ben,' she continued. 'What have you been telling him? At pre-school on Monday he told the supervisor that the nursery bookshelf needed to be thicker because strength or something varied with the thickness.'

'With its cube,' corrected Paul.

Debbie's face showed her exasperation. Her ex had been, as usual, seduced by the technology, missing the bigger picture completely. 'You've just demonstrated the point, he's four bloody years old. I want him to be a normal, happy, sociable little boy, not some childhood freak. The absolute last thing I want him to be is a smaller version of you.' Her ex-husband looked blankly at her, as if somehow switched off. She had experience with this side of him though, and he wasn't going to escape that way this time. 'And what have you been feeding him? He's been sick after the last two access days - peas and some sort of meat in a rich sauce. Four-year-olds need something simple to eat. Take him to McDonald's, kick a ball about, be normal, be like other bloody fathers.'

She'd obviously exhausted herself for the moment but still he couldn't think of anything to say. He'd fed Ben the same meal again, and surely the boy was bound to mention molecules. Christ.

Her ex-husband's attitude, that not-really-thereness, forced Debbie into twisting the knife further. 'I'm thinking of returning to the Family Court and applying to make your access less frequent. Supervised too. You'll be able to see Ben here, not alone on the boat.'

Still he didn't say anything, just soaking up the punches, what did I see in him, she wondered? 'Take this as a final warning, Paul. If you don't change within the next month I will apply to the court.'

Christ. He's on probation, he's a wrongdoer, he's being replaced by MGBman. Williams the Worthless. Still silent he turned for his bike and Debbie had a sudden memory of a coral reef.

Five or six years ago in the less financially restricted ClanCo era they and another couple, Colin and Pat, had chartered a yacht in Fiji, by far their most expensive holiday. Too many piña coladas at the Musket Bay Yacht Club had led them to attempt to return to their base mooring at the wrong time of day. Safe sailing in these sparsely buoyed waters requires the sun behind you so that reefs can be identified by the change in water colour. Or if there's enough wind you may be able to tell shallow water by the change in wave pattern. The most dangerous time to navigate is in calm water with the sun low in front of you, when water looks uniformly dull regardless of depth, as it was that day. Paul was confident that he knew the way back and had ordered the hoisting of the most awkward to handle sail, the spinnaker, to catch the zephyr coming from behind them. Half an hour later there was an awful graunching, grinding sound as the yacht impaled herself on a reef, coral heads now only too clear below them. For a few seconds Paul stood motionless, looking at the horizon as Debbie and Pat went into action looking for leaks in the cabin and Colin hassled the spinnaker untidily down. They found no immediate leaks and soon the three of them took to the dinghy while Paul managed to winkle the now slightly lighter yacht off the reef accompanied by more graunching noises. All crew back on board, they continued under engine with Colin and Pat at the bow looking ahead and one side each, Debbie with eyes on the depth sounder and Paul at the helm. Engine on tickover, they'd managed the mile or so back to their base without further mishap. Wearing mask and snorkel Paul found that the damage was limited to a few scars on the keel. They'd been very lucky. Later that evening, while they were playing cards, Paul asked if they had seen that horse on shore when the yacht was on the reef. Colin and Pat assumed he was joking but Debbie knew better, or was it worse? There had been no horse, nor had there been a shore in sight in the direction Paul was looking. She'd seen this before, under extreme stress Paul had for the first few seconds transferred himself to a world with which he could cope rather than deal with the immediate reality. At the time Debbie had asked herself if this transferred time would grow, and was this inherited or learnt behaviour? For Ben's sake, please let it not be inherited.

In the moment before Debbie closed the door Paul heard Ben's laughter from deep within the house.

Shortly after he sat in the cabin with no recollection of getting from Ben's house to the boat. All he could think about was Ben's laughter coming at the end of his utter defeat by Debbie. It was some time before his rational side had a chance to be listened to. His son laughed easily because his father had taken him home happy. Although the laughter came at the wrong time for his father there was nothing disloyal about it, it's just how a happy boy behaves.

But what was he going to do? Paul's natural tendency was to work in extremes, and he indulged himself now. One option might be to change his current life altogether. Get a job in Scotland or Cornwall and let Ben grow up without his birth father, become whatever product of nature and nurture he became. If, when an adult, he sought his father then Paul would meet him and discuss the reasons for abandoning all responsibility except for financial support, which he'd continue until Ben was an adult.

Or the other extreme, snatch Ben and sail off over

the horizon. Appealing though this was in his current mood, it wouldn't be possible. It needed money he didn't have to make the necessarily swift exit work. At the very least he'd need another boat in, say Falmouth, well provisioned and ready to sail at a moment's notice.

The lack of any spare cash meant the last option was out of the question. In fact, both were ridiculous. Just mental exercises to ease the pain. He'd have to try to be what his ex-wife wants. For the moment.

He glanced at the clock, 7:40 p.m. When Ben was here, he'd noticed that Sandpiper's water tank was low. There was time to row to Ferry Stores, fill the jerry cans, return and top up the tank before it got dark, he realised. Hurt, humiliation and despair were not fleeting emotions, he knew. They circle destructively and the exercise of rowing would provide a necessary something else to concentrate on for the moment. It wasn't until he was getting the oars out that he remembered Gunton's 'invitation' to meet at 8 at the White Hart.

The pub was at the other end of the village so he would certainly be late. If he bothered to go that is - he always enjoyed the 20-minute row to use the store's outside water tap, but he was not in his normal state. It's the pub, he decided. He'd see what Gunton and whoever else made up the 'they' have to say - was it only yesterday afternoon that they'd spoken outside the chandlers? It seemed much longer.

A little after eight on a Thursday evening was not one of the White Hart's lively times. Only six or seven people were in the main bar. He saw Gunton and another man sitting in a far corner. Gunton motioned Paul to sit opposite them. 'This is Jan,' he said, pronouncing the man's name Yan. Paul said his own name and offered his hand which the unsmiling Jan shook with the minimum possible touch. Lifelong friends were obviously not about to be made; this was business he realised.

'Adnams?' asked Gunton, turning for the bar without waiting for an answer, which left Paul with the thus far silent Jan, who was making no attempt to hide his scrutiny of the newcomer. Paul forced himself to look at Jan in turn. Probably about the same size as himself, forties, rugged weather-beaten complexion, fair hair, he looked like a proper sailor rather than a Mermaid Cove Marina one.

They continued to look at each other. Like two boxers before the start of a fight, trying to gain the mental ascendency, Paul thought. 'So, your boat,' Jan finally spoke, in good English with a Dutch or Flemish accent. 'Both outboard engines are reliable?'

Most boats of Sandpiper's class had a diesel engine. Unbeknown to Paul this man must have looked at his boat in sufficient detail to know that Sandpiper has her larger outboard engine in a cockpit well and the smaller spare one on a bracket at the stern. Paul would not have been able to afford Sandpiper if she'd had the more usual diesel. 'They have given no trouble so far. They don't get a lot of use as I try to sail as much as possible, why do you ask?'

Gunton placed the pint on the table. Paul thanked him and turned to Jan, expecting an answer but it was Gunton who spoke. 'When are you heading for Holland?'

Chandlery chatter, it had to be. Things mentioned there get swiftly distributed it seemed. 'If I go it's likely to be around mid-July. It's time you told me what's going on.' His attempt at assertiveness lacked conviction.

'We think you will be interested in delivering a few packages from Holland to somewhere on the Norfolk Broads. For this you will be paid very well,' said Jan.

'I'm getting by,' replied Paul, realising as he said it how defensive and weak it sounded.

Jan said. 'At ten thousand pounds a delivery you could sail off and restart your life elsewhere after two trips. You are bright enough to learn a new language quickly.'

'Take your son with you,' added Gunton.

Paul, startled by the amount Jan offered and the speed with which they'd got to this point, found himself asking. 'Why me, you must know I've never done anything like this?'

Gunton was obviously the junior of the two, it was Jan who continued in his precise English. 'Why you? Because neither you nor your boat look up to the part, but we think you are capable of making the passage in reasonable weather. And you have enough vacation to wait for good weather. You will make it look as if you have been sailing in the Orwell area by apparently coming up the coast to enter the Broads through Lowestoft. You will be met and unloaded somewhere between Lowestoft and here. Then you will continue to your mooring, clean and ten thousand pounds richer.'

'Is there any point in my asking what's in the packages? And what makes you think I won't go straight to the police?'

'It is not necessary to know. If you are stupid enough to go to the police you will find that this conversation never happened. If it comes to it there are two of us and we will say that you approached us saying that you were writing a book and wanted some background. You had picked the wrong people of course but we humoured you for as long as it takes to drink a pint. Then we asked you to leave. Later, when things have gone quiet again you will be in danger of being the victim of a boating accident. And, we know which boy is yours.'

'Tragic,' added Gunton, unnecessarily, Jan's words

and cool assurance were enough to convince Paul that he was completely out of his depth.

'So, my choices are either option one,' Paul searched for the right word, 'help with the delivery or option two, regard this evening as one where three boating folk had a pint together and I was asking you about sailing in the Ijsselmeer.'

'That sums it up well,' Jan replied. 'And when you leave now thank me very much for the background, shake hands and go. Acknowledge the bar staff on the way out. Look like a happy man who has just enjoyed a pint with newly made friends.'

Paul could not bring himself to say no outright. What does that say about me, he wondered? Nor could he say yes. 'I'll need to think about it,' he eventually said.

Gunton took over. 'I'll be here at 8 on Monday evening. Now make your exit as Jan told you to. And, for what it's worth, I don't smoke.'

Paul was sufficiently together to play the required role. As he waved thanks to the landlord the pub clock showed he'd been there only twenty minutes. 'Twenty minutes that changed a life,' he muttered dramatically to himself on the slow walk back to Sandpiper.

Small packages? Obviously, nothing live - Sandpiper may have to wait some days for weather safe enough to make the 104 nautical mile passage from Ijmuiden, the seaport of Amsterdam, so it could not be illegal immigrants or trafficked children - that would need a much bigger and quicker boat. Thinking himself glad it wasn't people he had to carry he realised he was already thinking like a criminal, though this didn't seem to stop him. What about exotic animals? He suddenly snorted, thinking of poor Sandpiper running out of wind for days in the middle of the North Sea and himself being eaten by a rare breed of hungry crocodile. What would this do for Ben's psyche, his criminal father coming to a deserved end? Or the opposite of course, in the middle of the windless North Sea he ran out of food and had to eat some of the exotic animals? The modern equivalent of the Horse Latitudes, the doldrums where ancient mariners having run out of normal food would start eating their more useful livestock. Sorry Mr Gunton, I had to eat your Himalayan Sun Parrot.

He forced himself away from this decoy activity. It had to be something like drugs, diamonds or stolen high value jewellery to justify ten thousand pounds. He didn't give a damn about silly adornments like jewellery though he'd still be a criminal if arrested. It was more likely to be drugs and he'd be in prison for decades if caught. Ben would grow up without him, the criminal father, an unbearable thought. And, if Gunton doesn't smoke, who was it at the gate the other night?

It was the morning to be standing shamefaced in front of the principal lecturer. At 8:55 a.m. Paul knocked on and opened the door marked.

PRINCIPAL LECTURER
ACCOUNTING STUDIES
G T TYSON BCom MA FCA

Caroline, Tyson's secretary, greeted him with less than her usual amount of warmth and indicated a seat. It was twenty minutes later when he entered the inner office by which time he'd come up with the fifth followed by the sixth revision of what he would say.

The principal lecturer remained seated at his desk. 'Good morning Paul. Don't take a seat, this will only take a few minutes.'

So, this is it, he thought, standing awkwardly, the end of my brief teaching career approaches rapidly.

'As you doubtless know, I had a deputation from your class. For the moment I'll ignore the copyright aspect of what you did but in any case, it was clearly wrong to give the students that sort of reading so close to their examinations,' said Tyson.

Paul's head was nodding as Tyson continued. 'After the exams you, your principal lecturer and I will discuss where to go from here. In the meantime, Caroline has photocopied twenty prints each of three past examination papers. With the class I want you to work through one set of papers in each of the three remaining weeks. Just to be clear, in your three sessions per week, each of one and a half hours duration, you are to work through with the class the answers to all eight questions on that week's paper. Eight questions per week. The following week, the same again with a different past exam paper. I know you are up to it technically and we have just organised things for you, so let's see it happen. Are you clear about what you have to do for the next three weeks?'

'Yes, quite clear,' Paul replied. He'd been treated like a disorganised dolt which, he presumed, was exactly what they thought he was.

'Caroline has the papers You have an hour or so before the first class to get a couple of answers organised.' Tyson looked down at his desk indicating it was time for Paul to leave.

Caroline did not speak but pointed to a stack of photocopies on a side table. Thanking her, Paul picked up the papers and walked back to the staffroom, part of him trying (and failing) not to feel small, part of him knowing that he'll have only about 40 minutes to come up with some answers that will stand up to what will surely be hostile scrutiny. Scanning quickly through the papers he found one with three questions he could answer with no great preparation. He made a pile of 20 copies of this paper then concentrated on making notes about the three questions he'd deal with today.

Entering class trying to appear more confident than he was he realised that three students were missing. A predictable three, he thought, and it's their loss.

'For each of the next three weeks I'll hand out a past examination paper on the Friday and work through with you the answers to two or three questions. We'll deal with the rest of this paper's questions on the following Monday and Wednesday. The rubric says that you have three hours in which to answer five questions of your choice from the eight presented on the paper, but we will deal with all eight of them. This OK with you?'

There were murmurings of yes and his confidence grew a little. Smiling at Adebola, Paul handed him fifteen copies of the paper of the week. 'Take one and pass on please. I'll give you ten minutes to decide which five questions you would attempt.'

During these ten minutes he saw that some of the stronger students were making notes about each question while others sat looking horrified. He knew that it would be a mistake to ask out loud which five questions they would answer thereby providing the weaker students with an opportunity to say they couldn't answer any, their teacher's fault of course.

After ten minutes Paul picked up a felt tip pen ready to write on the whiteboard. 'Question one then.

We are told that we work for a major airline which has eight new aircraft on order. The Marketing Department have made a case for more seats than originally planned for the new aircraft. Their case is based on an analysis of anthropometric data. Knowing how sharp you are at this sort of thing the Chief Accountant has passed this data on to you asking if the case has been made - the Marketing Department say that their aircraft layout will be able to seat all adult females and 98% of all adult males'.

'It's tempting to respond with questions of your own such as *what happens to the 2% who can't be seated* or *ah but they don't mean comfortably seated do they?* However, this is an exam and we need to put these thoughts aside and concentrate on finding a way through the mass of information the question provides. There is something quite realistic about the question in that there's a whole pile of information and what we have to do is recognise what is relevant and what is not. In the course we have covered fully the techniques needed to answer the question. In fact, it's a straightforward one if you de-clutter it and see what is needed. So ... who's seen what's needed?'

Immediately after asking that Paul wondered if he'd been foolish. A few seconds of silence passed, and he was about to acknowledge failure and answer the question himself when Emma raised her hand. Thank heavens, she's about to rescue him again.

'Emma,' Paul said.

'The dimension that will most determine seat layout is the small of the back to the knee and, if we assume that this dimension is normally distributed, then the only measures relevant are the arithmetic mean and the standard deviation of that dimension.'

Paul replied, laughing with pleasure. 'Emma is not only brave to be the first one to answer but she's also absolutely correct.' He could see a number of the brighter ones nodding, wanting him to understand that they too were on the right path.

'All the measures such as range, mode and the such given in the question are not relevant if we quite reasonably assume that figures for the small of the back to the knee are normally distributed,' Paul continued. 'So, look at the normal distribution table attached to your formula sheet. When the Marketing Department say 98% of all adult males, do they mean all except for the top and bottom 1%?'

The class was fully with him now, a number of voices answered. 'No, no they mean excluding the tallest 2% of all adult males.'

'But what about females?' Paul asked.

'It is always worth considering them,' replied Briony with almost a smile.

'Essential,' agreed Paul. Recognising that he was on safe ground now he worked through the mechanics of the answer on the whiteboard, finding that the Marketing Department's figures held up, just.

The session became almost jolly as they decided that none of the Harlem Globetrotters basketball team would fit in the Marketing Department's seating scheme, they presumably trotted the globe in their own aircraft with much more space between seats. Paul did not move on to question two until the approximately even distribution of female and male students in the class started to josh each other about other physical differences unmentioned in question one's data. Question two concerned probability and was, in principle, similar to its predecessor in that more information was given than was necessary to come up with the correct answer. Paul supposed that the questions just reflected everyday life - somewhere amid all the clutter is the right thing to do. Somewhere. There were murmurings of 'thank you' as he finished the class. Success! If only he could have got there under his own steam instead of being kicked there by the principal lecturer.

Aboard Sandpiper later that evening the euphoria of his success with the accounting class had worn off. The blunt instrument of G T Tyson BCom MA FCA ETC had clearly shown what was expected of a teacher in this sort of college. Get them through their exams, nothing more and most certainly nothing less. It was the sort of occupation with long holidays that many would envy but did he have the stamina to stay doing this for another 30 years? And what about the Debbie access threat? And the Gunton/Jan proposition plus threat? The one certainty was that the cosy lifestyle of the last few months was over. He'd been enjoying what he thought was his simple life while oblivious to the pressures building on him. What a fool. Action was needed now. What had he told the class earlier today - somewhere, amid all the clutter, is the information you need to be able to come up with the right response? How very easy to say in relation to a forty-minute answer to an exam question, how difficult in real life. He needed a weekend in isolation. A weekend of reckoning while at anchor three miles away on Eastland Broad.

It was nearly 8 p.m., just time to motor gently downriver with the last of the ebb, topping up Sandpiper's water tanks at Ferry Stores on the way. In the last hour of daylight, the tree-lined banks of the Yare enclosed a peaceful world. He loved this time, this place - running at not much above tickover the soft burble of the Yamaha engine and the barely visible wake of the yacht as she moved slowly downriver, a boat seemingly at one with her environment. A feeling he shared; he'd have to be very unhappy to deliberately leave this area.

 A long narrow dyke led to Eastland Broad. They

turned into the dyke with its moored boats, many of them hire cruisers whose crews would be having their last night aboard before returning them to the boatyards in the morning. The fear of running aground and possibly blocking the engine's cooling system ensured that almost all boats moored alongside here in the dyke rather than anchoring in the shallow waters outside the broad's buoyed navigation channel. Entering the broad he saw that Sandpiper would be the sole boat at anchor tonight. Heaven.

It was about low water as Sandpiper nudged into the mud to the south of the channel. He walked forward and lowered the anchor, letting out five metres of chain. Back in the cockpit he set the engine astern for a few seconds to dig in the anchor, stirring up a great deal of mud in the process. The westerly to south-westerly winds were forecast to be light for the weekend so this short length of chain ought to be enough.

THREE
2019

Saturday morning on the broad, he lay abed trying not to start the weekend of reckoning. This lethargy continued when he eventually got up and sat eating toast in the cockpit, having spent at least five unnecessary minutes drying a spot which caught the morning sun. Washing up was normally an every two-day event and not due until tomorrow evening, but he did it this morning anyway, followed by a second mug of coffee while he watched birds, mostly swan and duck feeding, and pairs of grebe encroaching on or defending territory. Displacement activity ruled OK. A few other boats passed by in the channel. As usual, he studiously avoided the eye contact with their humans which tended to result in an obligation to wave - what was the point of isolating yourself on your mobile island and then indulging in this sort of social contact?

Perhaps he should give up teaching he thought, yet again. Or at least coaching for exams - but isn't most teaching ultimately for this? Probably, but he knows he's more suited to the backroom techie role, the job he filled at ClanCo not that many years ago. But of course, if he wasn't teaching it would be more difficult to follow Ben if Debbie moved elsewhere. Not many towns were awash with jobs requiring a detailed knowledge of vehicle assembly or the maths needed to analyse a factory layout. If he wanted to continue being an important person in Ben's life, then he had to continue teaching. Simple as that. His access was under threat, so he had to knuckle down, play the standard Sunday-father-with-son role. Grit his teeth, pretend to be Carlos Kickaball, famous striker for Dreamland United. Patronise McDonald's, etc, etc. The Debbie standard father.

But what about Ben's natural tendencies? Paul smiled, recalling Debbie's complaint about Ben advising the nursery manager on the thickness of their bookshelves. A couple of weeks ago on the boat Paul demonstrated deflection with a ruler, a thicker piece of wood and weights. He had not mentioned shelves, his son had seen the principle, not just the application. And he's only four! Paul thought back to what little he knew about his own father and grandfather, both dead now but he's been told that they had shown what we call these days nerdish, obsessive behaviour. How could he possibly leave Ben to be brought up by Debbie and MGBman alone. Ben had to be given the stimulus to suit the gifts he so clearly possessed. And this was down to Paul himself, Ben was due to start school in September and it was becoming clear that he wouldn't get all he needed as one of a class of thirty plus pupils in the local primary.

'Take your son with you,' Gunton said on Thursday evening. A snatch, a kidnap, an escape with his son. Once he started thinking about it, he couldn't stop.

'What is a perfect snatch?' he asked out loud, realising right away that the word perfect is inappropriate in this context. Even if perfectly executed from his viewpoint someone, more than one, would be hurt - obviously Debbie, her family and Paul's mother would be severely hurt, devastated is the word tabloids would use. And it would be tough for himself and Ben for a time. In the long term he knew that he'd be good for his son's development but how could he present this dramatic change to Ben? An adventure? God, that's weak, he'd have to think of something better than that.

If snatched there's no way Ben and himself could remain in the UK. You have to register for everything. They'd be caught within the week and that would be the end of access. No, a successful snatch would certainly mean moving to another country. But where? Which countries did not have an extradition treaty with the UK? And were any of these safe for a man and small boy? And did they have a language that would be reasonably quick to learn? Somewhere he could get a job, teaching English perhaps? It would almost certainly be somewhere beyond Europe.

Money. A successful snatch needed money and the only way he was going to get a significant amount would be doing a 'run' for Gunton & Co, and even then, would it be enough? If it was to be a boating escape, then they'd need something stronger than Sandpiper if the destination was beyond Europe. At the moment the pound sterling was weak against the euro so he couldn't buy a cheap but sound boat in, say, Spain and make a quick getaway. Buying a yacht in the UK and sailing off at somewhere around 5 knots (about 6mph) would not qualify for quick getaway status. What about buying one already close to somewhere like South America? He knew that yachts were occasionally sold cheaply in places like Panama or the Caribbean when, after an Atlantic crossing, their crews decided that ocean sailing was not for them. They'd accept something well below normal value just to be able to walk (fly more likely) away from it all. He suddenly recalled that one of his old ClanCo colleagues, Steve Johnson, had copped out four or five years ago now and was, he'd heard, living a water gypsy's life on his catamaran in St Georges, Grenada, only a few days sailing from South America. Grenada was a smallish island; it shouldn't be difficult to get in touch with Steve. Perhaps he'd know of a decent boat going cheap as its owners decided they couldn't continue. Since Steve was already living in the margins, he may be happy to help without wanting to know every detail. Would he be able to get a boat for, say, £5,000?

The problem with flights of course is that they are documented so any flight to, say Grenada, would be easily traced. So, how can a man and young boy travel incognito? Within the UK it was still possible to pay cash for a bus or train ticket so they could get to somewhere on the UK's south coast within eight hours. If they had a ready-to-go yacht in, say Portsmouth, then they could be offshore within a few hours of leaving Ben's home. It was feasible he thought, but only if he could extend access to eight hours. He'll have to play the father role Debbie described, or proscribed. A day on the beach in Yarmouth or Lowestoft during the summer holiday was the obvious answer. He'd have to work towards picking up Ben at 9 a.m., catching the train to the beach and then have him home by 5 p.m. This would have to work well for a couple of occasions then on the planned day they'd catch the train to the city, National Express bus to London, National Express bus to Portsmouth then local bus to a marina where a well prepared and stocked yacht lay ready to head out into the channel. By the time the police had missing person forms filled in he and Ben would be heading south watching the Isle of Wight growing smaller. Mid channel, about forty miles from both the UK and France they'd turn west and head for the Atlantic.

He drifted on, thinking of where a first landfall might be until he realised that he'd become distracted. A few more lines of that cycling poem/verse or whatever it was had unconsciously formed ...

> My way is alight
> With the red and white
> Of empty fast food boxes
> Empty as the sincerity
> Of the face on their top
>
> Night revellers sowed this crop

... he wrote the words down, useless as they were to the current problem then laughed as he imagined lawyers for the relevant fast food company squirming with delight as they went into attack mode. Night revellers though? How old was he, 80? There had to something better than that, (clubbers?) or avoid the necessity, perhaps simply

> Who sowed this crop
> Scattered hastily at random
> To degrade at length?

I have no answer, I am
A Sunday father with son
Canvas for a child's colour
Provider of fun

Yet again displacement activity had taken over. The poet of the back lane into the city! He wrenched himself back to the weekend of reckoning. Up to this point he'd just been responding to things as they happen, surely it was now time to be proactive rather than continue as a responder? If he allowed things to continue, then Ben wouldn't fulfil his potential.

But why wouldn't he fill his potential? Who was Paul Williams to say that Ben won't? He probably wouldn't fulfil it with Debbie alone but what about MGBman? His car had been at the former matrimonial home a number of times now. What was the man's background? Paul resolved to find out something about him. He'd been reluctant to do this, not wanting to involve Ben in a squalid *this man is staying overnight, he should be part paying for the former matrimonial home* sort of dispute.

The wind had been a gentle westerly, there was high pressure over Spain. In a brief return to the present tense he realised that the sun was now in line with Sandpiper's engine. A glance at the clock showed that it was after 5 p.m. The day had moved on while he sat thinking, enjoying, if that's the right word, his weekend of reckoning. Instead of a late lunch he decided to make do with an early evening meal.

At dusk he sat in the cockpit with the day's final mug of coffee watching a flock of gulls gathering on the far side of the broad where they settled for a night afloat. Starlings gathered in the air, rising and swooping above the broad as the size of the flock increased by the minute. Twenty or so flying in from one direction and thirty from another until the flock now numbering high hundreds, perhaps a thousand, swept with a whoosh down past Sandpiper to roost for the night in the reeds just metres away. A wonderful display, how could he bear to leave this place? This place where he has the privilege of being the sole human among the birds of the broad.

Thus, relaxed, he didn't take a sleeping pill and as a result found his mind flickering inconclusively over his problems for what seemed like a long time. It was after 8 a.m. when he woke, happy from a dream in which he'd become a blond, blue eyed 26-year-old hunk with an engineering PhD. His work partner was a beautiful female cat who was an aerodynamicist specialising in the recovery and reuse of vortex energy. Only he could communicate with her. They'd gone to work for the Williams formula one team where he developed an engine mode which made the car very quick indeed in qualifying and the cat had designed the aerodynamics such that the car was not only slippery through the air but almost impossible to overtake due to the wild airflow behind it - her superior feline sense of balance finding the maximum benefit point between these two opposing features. Blessed with this genius pair Williams won the world championship that year and Clare Williams fell head over heels for the hunk.

The happy Dr Blond Hunk glow lasted until he'd finished his toast when reality trod suddenly and heavily upon him. Decisions had to be made. He started to write down anything that related to where he was now and what were his options. Was there a critical path through to success - and what does success mean in this situation?

1. His four-hour unfettered access to Ben was under threat from Debbie.

2. His job was under threat due his own poor performance.

3. He was under threat from Gunton, Jan & Co who were trying to involve him in serious crime.

And none of these three was in isolation - he'd taken the teaching job to try to ensure access to Ben. His son was a potential victim of Gunton & Co. If caught in criminality his sentence would obviously prevent access to Ben.

He knew that Do Nothing was a viable option in

many situations though in this case the option meant do nothing drastic. In other words, continue as is but with some changes. If this is what he chose to do, then he'd have to ...

a. Knuckle down on access day and be the Debbie standard father model.

b. Knuckle down at college and be as close to the standard teacher model as he could manage.

c. Politely decline Gunton and Jan's 'offer' and convince them that he would never do anything to shop them.

d. Find a way of continuing some parts of his former simple life aboard Sandpiper - enjoy the evening row downriver for supplies - remove himself from the world by anchoring here on the broad for the weekend - be the Hermit of Davison's Dyke when he could.

Still with the Do Nothing option he wrote the heading Downsides ...

1. Access would always be subject to Debbie's whims. He wouldn't put it past her to use access to gain some form of revenge, she knows his life is centred on Ben. And access would have to change in September when Ben starts school. She could make that change a misery.

2. He may already be marked for the sack at college though they would be more likely to ask him to resign at the end of the term. If not this bad, then he

suspected he'd be allocated classes such as brick stacking patterns with Labourers Year 1. You have to be a certain sort of person to survive the teaching of that sort of class and he was not that person. The resulting unhappiness would soon filter through to his son.

3. Would Gunton & Co accept a thank you but no thank you answer? They spoke to him because they had him marked as vulnerable and needy. And he had a good chance of success because he looked and behaved like an amateur yachtie rather than a criminal. But would they accept the thank you but no thank you answer from someone they have already defined as vulnerable and needy when he said he'd never do anything to implicate them? Probably not, reliable does not equate with vulnerable and needy. The result could be Ben as a victim. Clearly the Do Nothing option was not on.

He'd already rejected as unthinkable just moving away to another part of the UK and not being part of Ben's childhood. It was probably not practical anyway. He'd still have to pay maintenance so would need to quickly find another job with a nearby cheap liveaboard mooring for Sandpiper. No, that's not an option either.

A Snatch? A Kidnap? An Escape with One's Son, Paul wrote, and almost immediately cursed himself. It was not a subject for levity even if it was done in an attempt to alleviate his feelings about this crude sledgehammer of an option.

He'd already convinced himself that they'd be found within the week if running to another part of the UK. This probably applied to other European countries as well though it might take a little longer to find them. He needed to find a faraway place which would provide a safe haven.

But how to get to this faraway place? In the next few weeks he'd have to work hard at getting access up to eight hours duration. At Ben's age it was never going to be more than eight. An airline can get you a long way in eight hours but of course it leaves an easily followed trail. Ferries from the UK only go to a limited number of European near neighbours and they don't do it quickly. There was a good chance they'd be stopped at an early border control. UK citizens do have one advantage though - there is no compulsory reporting of small craft traffic. Without having to notify anyone, Brits still have the right to head offshore in whatever ramshackle vessel they chose. This was the way. A seaworthy ready-to-go yacht in the Portsmouth area, reached by express coach, would succeed. The very slowness of the yacht's subsequent passage at 5 knots or so would be an asset. It would be a long time before they showed up anywhere. A missing, suspected snatched, child cannot continue to be front page news or the trending topic for long. There will always be a next big thing, and a next ...

Yes, this was the way forward he decided and started to write down the necessary steps.

1. Keep things ticking over at college with no hint of him leaving of his own accord.

2. Play the Debbie standard father role starting now. Make it clear she's won.

3. Starting in the last two weeks of term (when he had fewer classes) try to establish an eight-hour beach day with Ben.

4. Say yes to Gunton tomorrow night. It was the only way to get enough money to buy a small yacht seaworthy enough to cross an ocean.

5. Research potential safe destinations and the necessary passages to them.

6. Research small yachts for sale in the Portsmouth area. Portsmouth being chosen because they could get there in the access day timing. It was also in the Solent, the most populous sailing area of the country so there were usually plenty of boats for sale - with cash he might be in a good bargaining position. Once he'd bought a boat then he'd have somewhere in the area to stay while getting her ready to sail far.

Sitting back in the cockpit he thought once more of the Do Nothing option, the having to grit his teeth and play the roles necessary to continue access to Ben. He thought of his technique for bearing the short term unbearable, the move into the inner world he could cope with, the one inside his head. In the past, while a dentist did something nasty inside his mouth, in his mind he was sailing in French Polynesia trying to decide between the comparatively short distance to anchor in Bora Bora's lagoon or to sail further to a centre of Polynesian culture on Raiatea. On another occasion his head was in Polynesia again as a nurse practitioner pushed her flexible sigmoidoscope up his rear end looking for problems. In his ear her assistant described what was going on in soothing tones, encouraging him to look at the screen and be amazed by the complexity of his insides. But his eyes stayed shut, words about bowels and colons could not compete with the care needed to pass through the tricky buoyage into Papeete's harbour on Tahiti.

Putting himself into an inner world while being hurt required considerable willpower but he'd developed the technique early on as an asthmatic child, lying on his bed trying not to panic into worrying where the next breath was coming from, which would only make things worse. Instead, he was England's left sided striker, flicking the ball one way past an Argentinian defender while spinning around him in the other and volleying a pass straight onto the head of

Alan Shearer who scored the winning goal. Thinking about it now he realised that even at that young an age, in an inner world where there were no restrictions, he'd almost always played the role of hero's helper rather than the hero. A team player, an avoider of the limelight. Someone not quite the real deal?

Across the broad gulls were gathering for the night, seen yet unseen as his thoughts on imagined worlds strayed from the fit enough to be an international footballer to the other extreme. To the common image of an old peoples' home and its dayroom, TV blaring in the corner, unwatched by residents with vacant expressions. Away with the fairies we say but perhaps they were away in their own more congenial scenarios - walking the dog on the moor - looking at their smart selves in the mirror before a big night out - anywhere but where their bodies are at present. He smiled, realising that winning the formula one championship with his aerodynamicist cat friend was certainly on the away-with-the-fairies level. In his dream she was a beautiful grey tabby with blue eyes and if this was what fairies looked like then roll on being away with them. And, thinking on, if caught doing a 'run' for Gunton & Co this inner world may be the only way of surviving imprisonment. If he wanted to survive.

At the end of Monday's accounting class Emma

stayed behind long enough for the two of them to be alone in the room.

'What about tomorrow, 5:30 p.m., Union Street Costa?' she asked.

'OK, I'll look forward to seeing you there,' he replied.

They smiled at each other, in some complicity? Was he about to embark on a further error of judgement? For another two weeks or so she was still one of his students and, subject to an external assessment, he was also her subject examiner. Add in the fact that she was married and a NoGo sign (three of them perhaps) should be flashing in front of his eyes. Or they would have been a couple of weeks ago but now the ground seems to have shifted underneath him.

Monday evening. Gunton and Jan sat at the same table as before in the sparsely occupied pub. Wanting to avoid starting as the supplicant Paul walked over to them and said, in what he hoped came across as confidence. 'My round I believe.'

Both men nodded in agreement. 'Two pints of Ghost Ship,' said Jan.

Leaning close to them as he put their drinks on the table, Paul said quietly. 'I'll do two trips.' Gunton responded by trying and failing to suppress an I-knew-it smirk. Bastard.

Jan reached down and produced a large and

colourful booklet of papers and said in his precise English, 'I will lend you two items to make your holiday cruise a success. And I will run you through places you should visit and show you some good overnight anchorages.'

Handing over the booklet Jan added. 'This is Dutch chart folio 1800 which covers the Ijsselmeer, Randmeer and Noordzeecanaal.'

Reaching down once more he came up with a large padded mail envelope and continued. 'And I will also lend you my booklets covering bridge and lock opening schedules and their vhf contact channels. They are in this envelope.'

'The envelope also contains a dual sim mobile on pay as you go. We have both numbers and we'll call you when arrangements need to be made, here or in Holland,' Gunton added in a low voice then continued. 'I've also installed a Navionics Europe charting app and Windfinder Pro weather forecasting. The Navionics is battery hungry so make sure your boat has an always-on USB socket.'

'OK,' replied Paul. It was a lot to take in. And the bastards must have been confident he'd say yes.

Jan moved to Paul's side of the table and spread the chart folio on the floor. Opening the folio, he started to talk Paul through the places he should visit - Edam, Marken, Hoorn then through the lock into the Ijsselmeer at Enkhuizen. 'Enkhuizen has the

Zuider Zee Museum (Jan said Zowder Zay Museum and Paul logged to memory this proper pronunciation) and you can anchor here.' Jan pointed to a spot immediately to the south of the museum where he'd marked a circle with a dot inside it, like an old school navigator's position estimate with its potential error circle.

'One of the two places we will make contact,' Jan said in a low voice. 'The other is here.' He pointed to a similarly marked place south of Durgerdam. 'Do not go into Durgerdam harbour, anchor outside among the barges which often wait here between loads.'

Talking once more at normal volume Jan proved a more than competent tour guide, explaining the merits of visiting the two old Dutch East India Company ports of Hoorn and Enkhuizen, saying that he should also visit some Friesland towns (Harlingen, Hindeloopen ...) and to make sure he tried a brown plate meal and a rijstaffel.

'You really mean some of this, don't you? You certainly know your country,' Paul said, smiling.

Smiling in return, Jan said, 'You can always tell a Dutchman.' Then, after a small delay he added, 'But you can't tell him much.'

'So I've heard,' Paul laughed.

This bonhomie was too much for Gunton, this was not how it should be, the bloody man was about to be their mule. 'To get serious again, what date are you leaving for the cruise?' he asked.

'Around the 15th of July,' Paul replied. 'That's six days after college ends.'

They had finished their second pint, and this seemed to bring an end to proceedings, so Paul held up the folio and the envelope, thanked the two men and promised to keep in touch, and to return the borrowed items at the end of the cruise. Waving thanks to the landlord he left the pub and walked back to Sandpiper, mind racing with thoughts of using the mobile for untraceable research on safe destinations for himself and Ben.

A young Dutch woman, Anneke Wilders, worked in ColComp, a recently bestowed snappy name which failed to supply the hoped-for lift in status of the not quite up to date college computer department. If he bought the sandwiches Anneke agreed to spend twenty minutes of her lunch break teaching him conversational Dutch. The first session on Tuesday turned out to be enjoyable for both of them, particularly his spluttering attempt at saying Scheveningen. Anneke also recommended the free online Speak Dutch course run by the University of Groningen. He signed up for this on the college computing system at the end of his last class. Progress was definitely being made.

Oke Anneke. Dank je wel. Tot ziens! (OK

Anneke. Thank you very much. See you!)

After college he and Emma met at the coffee house. 'Can I say how well your last two sessions have gone with us? Most of the class are feeling they'll do OK or better in your subject,' she opened.

'Please feel free to say it frequently!' he replied, smiling broadly.

'I invited you so the first coffee is on me, how do you like it?'

'Strong and black, so double shot americano please,' he responded, noting her use of the word first - there were to be more perhaps, a hardship he was sure would be bearable.

At college since their last meeting he had started noticing her slim figure in jeans and a sweatshirt lightweight enough to just show a hint of a nipple outline, or two he corrected himself. He looked at her now as she stood waiting at the counter, a good shape, definitely a fanciable lady.

Coffee on the table in front of them, they looked at each other and smiled once more. Again, she was the first to speak. 'I can't think of any indirect way of starting this, so I'll risk coming right out with it. I would like to see more of you.'

She continued to look straight at him, without apparent embarrassment. You don't get any more direct than that, he imagined. 'The feeling is mutual but what about your husband?'

'We still share a house but that's all. Once I qualify, I'll move to find a practice which will take me on as a junior partner, then we'll divorce.'

'Please call me Paul. As you probably know, I'm divorced with a four-year-old son and live on my own on my scruffy yacht in an isolated place six miles away. Prospects are things other men have.'

'I'm not looking for long term commitments, Paul, but I would like to know you in every sense of the word. I can come to you on the yacht.'

'You are wonderfully direct; I feel refreshed just being with you.'

'I've wanted to talk like this and be close to you for a long time but I know that relationships between staff and students are verboten. But if I leave it any longer, we could easily lose touch and I don't want that to happen.'

'There are the Thursday afternoons with my son, Ben, but other than that I don't have regular meetings beyond classroom ones.'

'Then you are perfectly placed for a married woman to ensnare, and I shall do so,' she said, laughing before adding, 'it's just a question of when.'

'This is incredible. You have been sitting in my class for what, eight months now? Working hard, making valid comments, the perfect mature student.

And here you are right this minute, in control of how our interaction is going. It's a role reversal and I'm impressed and thoroughly enjoying it. Let the promised ensnaring commence asap.'

'I have a small car. It might be a good idea if, after you're finished teaching for the day, you walk down to this place then when you see my car stop outside you hop in and we go to your boat for the night. I'll drop you back within walking distance of the college the following morning. And we'll do this on a couple of days a week when our classroom schedules are at their most convenient. Should anyone notice us together then we'll say I'm driving you to meet my husband who has expressed an interest in sailing and is therefore taking advantage of my being in contact with you.'

'You have put a lot of thought into this.'

'It shows how much I'd like to be with you. Despite being a Norfolk born girl I've never had a night aboard a boat, nor made love on one. These are not omissions, they're faults needing to be rectified.'

'Tell me when the first of your fault rectifications will occur and I will be sure to prepare a supper you will remember followed, I hope, by a night to remember.'

'Monday and Wednesday are good for me. I can't make tomorrow, but shall we meet on Monday next week, 5:30 here?'

'I'll go for that. In fact, I'll go back now and start scrubbing the boat so she's ready to receive you on Monday.' He leaned forward aiming to kiss her on the cheek, but she saw it coming and turned her head such that they kissed on the lips. 'Bad girl, thank heavens,' he told her quietly then got up and left.

Near to Davison's Dyke was a maze of shallow water channels unsuitable for any boat larger than a human powered one. On Tuesday early evening he rowed Sandpiper's battered tender deep into the maze, eventually tethering the dinghy to a clump of reeds. He had rowed here on his first post-divorce Christmas Day. Then, a flask of tea, two mince pies and a tangerine formed what a bystander might regard as a particularly meagre lunch. The same bystander would perhaps see a man in need of some Christmas cheer but in fact he was revelling in his freedom to behave that way. The simplicity of his Christmas meal was its virtue and he ate it here among the other creatures for whom this was just another day, one to survive. It was also one of his earliest days playing the role of the Hermit of Davison's Dyke, a simple life now shattered by Briony, Debbie and Gunton, to put faces to the present threats.

And, welcome as it was in many ways, there was the added complication of Emma. On Monday in the coffee house he'd been stupid enough to mention a night to remember. An easy few words to say but, for a man as far out of practice as he was, achieving something memorable would almost certainly be difficult. He ought to tell her that he won't be able to cope with the pressure, flattering though it was to be her sex object.

And was it really only a few days ago that he thought he was happy living a simple life?

He was in the village chandlery again in the late afternoon of the following day. In the shop also was an elderly woman he'd seen before, both in the village and in here, an American. Elderly yes, and a little on the chubby side but looking undeniably cute in denim top and faded blue dungarees. Real sailing people just stand out, they're instantly recognisable as different from Mermaid Cove Marina ones he reminded himself. They left the shop together and when the chandlery door shut, she asked if he was Paul Williams. 'Yes,' he replied, smiling.

'I'm Rose Bailey. I've been wanting to talk to you, well ... proposition you actually,' she said with a broad smile.

'I keep getting propositioned, must change my aftershave,' he joked.

'Your aftershave is just fine, I'm sure. I know you have a long vacation and I'd like to ask if you would consider helping me to take my yacht to the Canaries during your vacation. She's a forty-two-foot Choy Lee clipper, ketch rigged and in very good order. I am able to pay for help.'

A Choy Lee forty-two-footer was a £100,000 plus yacht, Paul's shock must have been obvious as Rose Bailey continued. 'I've got my car here, come and see her, she's in the Mermaid Cove Marina.'

'I thought they were all gin palaces there,' he said, continuing in jokey mode.

'Only ninety nine percent of them, come and see one of the exceptions.'

He entered the chandlery again and asked if he could leave his bike at the back of the shop. No problem he was assured.

Sitting in the car they had to wait ten minutes for the railway gates to open during which Rose explained that a couple of years ago Haley, her granddaughter, and Haley's USAF officer husband, Lee, had been posted to Mildenhall, about fifty miles from the village. Then in her mid-seventies Rose decided to have one final adventure so hired a crew and sailed her yacht from the Chesapeake Bay area to here, about as close to Mildenhall as a large sea going yacht could get. Now that Lee was about to be posted back to the USA, this summer was the time to enact the second half of Rose's final adventure. She wanted to be in the Canaries in July or August. She'd wait there until mid-November before the return crossing of the Atlantic, and she already had someone lined up for that part.

'So, I just need help to the Canaries. I will pay all the boat expenses, your airfare home plus one thousand pounds. How does that sound?'

'Very inviting indeed,' he replied, the back of his mind working hard on the logistics. If he was truly well organised and the weather was kind, he could get in two 'runs' to Holland plus the Canaries passage during the holidays and be £21,000 better off. And he'd also be a criminal.

'How did you know I was a potential helper?' he asked.

'Here-say and chandlery chatter,' she replied.

Rose's yacht lay at the far end of the Mermaid Cove Marina, near the river. The proverbial swan compared with the plastic ducks surrounding her. Lovingly crafted in Hong Kong in the late 1980s and bought by Rose in Macau in 1992, she was everything a sailor could desire. Heaven could be defined as being paid to handle this beauty. The yacht's name was Audacity, should he be brave (audacious, not brave) and say yes right now?

He held off doing that and asked Rose about her background learning that she was a former foreign correspondent, the Kate Adie of my time, as she described herself.

'I do know of Kate Adie,' he said. 'My mother is a regular listener to the BBC radio programme From Our Own Correspondent.'

Rose lit her third cigarette in the short time they had been together. He supposed it was not surprising that she smoked heavily, she must have been in some tight spots in her earlier career. Suddenly it twigged, the other night at the gate.

'Were you smoking by the gate to Davison's Dyke around 11 p.m. sometime last week?'

'Yes, I was feeling restless and couldn't sleep so I thought I'd check out where I'd been told you lived. When I saw you come out, I thought at first I'd walk over and introduce myself then realised that it wasn't appropriate at that hour. So, I saw you in the chandlers this afternoon and took my opportunity.'

FOUR

2019

At first glance the good clipper Audacity seemed awash with oiled hardwood, her decks laid with elegantly curved strips of teak, looking far too good to carelessly walk on. Paul took off his shoes and padded around, noting that all sail handling had to be done at the masts where large, ocean weight sails and thick ropes ensured that this was not a yacht which would be easy to sail singlehanded. He turned to face Rose. 'As it will take some time to get all four sails up and trimmed, then probably as long again to stow them properly, can I take it that we would not be day sailing our way along the English coast?'

'Oh no, once she's sailing well, we'll keep going until we're tired, ideally making Falmouth in one passage. We can have a couple of days rest there, stock up with fresh food then head out into the Atlantic when the weather suits. If Great Yarmouth to Falmouth is too long a passage, then we could stop at Brighton maybe.' She looked at him with a questioning expression on her face.

'I'm happy to do two or three hours on, two or three off for as long as it takes,' he replied, a statement whose substance amounted to nothing but bravado since he hadn't sailed a passage that long before. Where were these statements coming from? Here he was, playing the role of experienced passage maker with Rose and the role of experienced and available lover with Emma. Perhaps this was all he amounted to - a person whose major focus was on having a good interaction, he'd say what he thinks the other person wants to hear. Play the required part. A man for all seasons. Billy Liar.

With an effort he put aside his self-doubt and went down below. Here, Audacity was sheer luxury typified by buttoned-leather seating of about six inches depth, Sandpiper having a spartan three inches. Oddly though, the gleaming teak and glass drinks cabinet contained just one bottle of blackcurrant cordial. Seeing his surprise at this meagre fare she told him that despite the apparent luxury of her surroundings she lived a relatively austere life, mostly for the sake of her health.

Avoiding subsequent mention of her smoking he continued an inspection of the cabin noticing pilot berths high up on both sides of the saloon. He looked for and found their leecloth fixing points prompting Rose to say. 'On passage we can use the pilot berths to hot bunk if that's OK with you.'

'Absolutely fine,' he replied, thinking that if he accepted her proposition then he'd be sharing a bed with Rose, but not in the everyday sense of the expression.

'Rose, Audacity is the most beautiful yacht and I'm sure that you and I will get on well. I am therefore tempted to say yes and let everything else fall into place but I'm going to be sensible and ask for one week to see how I can arrange the things I want to do this summer,' Paul said.

'That's what I expected and I'm looking forward to hearing from you,' she replied, adding with a smile, 'particularly if it's a yes!'

Rose offered to drive him back to the chandlers, but he said that he'd slowly amble back on foot taking an opportunity to look around the marina. They shook hands and he walked away thinking that he now had the perfect opportunity to openly research sailing to the Canaries and, in a spirit of helping Rose, openly research a subsequent Atlantic crossing.

Walking slowly toward the marina entrance he noted the class names of various gin palaces and sports boats - not the individual boat names but brands of the boats - Intruder 33, Marauder 38, Interceptor 29, Four Winns 27, Revenger 28 ... Revenger, Good God!

He resolved that if he won some gigantic sum then he'd buy a boatyard and make a range of boats which would be marketed as the Conciliator 33, Pacifist 38, Peacemaker 29, Five Losses 27 ... nobody would buy them of course, not the right image at all. Silliness then overtook him completely and he settled on producing the Peacemaker 32 with built-in dovecote. And he'd publish a magazine entitled Well 'Ard Sea Angler to advertise the Peacemaker in. It should go down well. He sniggered, how inappropriate for a boat the last thought was.

The boats here were not all gin palaces he noticed, there were a few exceptions other than Audacity. A good looking traditional Dutch steel cruiser lay ahead. At that moment the boat's starboard central cabin door slid open and, to his surprise, Jan ducked out onto deck, turned and saw Paul, and looked surprised in return. 'Have I the honour of a visit?' he asked.

'I've just been speaking with Rose on the Choy Lee ketch, Audacity,' he replied.

'Ah, lovely boat, lovely lady. Rose asked you for help her to the Canaries I expect.'

'Yes, how did you know?'

Instead of answering Jan said. 'Come aboard and have coffee. See what one of the other non gin palaces look like.'

Once inside Jan's boat the raised central cabin seemed larger than it had looked from the outside. There was an internal helm and controls on the port side plus seating on all the other sides except where cabin and deck access was needed. Pride of place in the centre was a table with a large pinboard on top. Pinned to this was an old-fashioned blueprint with an almost complete balsawood model aircraft wing above it. While Jan made coffee in the forward cabin Paul looked closely at the wing and its drawing below. Although it was about four feet long it was only half a wing. He recalled much smaller, simpler aircraft kits he'd assembled as a schoolboy. They were all very amateur hour compared with this one. 'This is a serious piece of kit, Jan. When it's assembled how will you get it out of the door?'

'I won't as such. If it had to go around as a complete aircraft it wouldn't go in my car either. Models this size are made to be quickly assembled when you want to fly them,' Jan replied.

'Presumably you can't fly it from the boat. Where do you go?'

'There are three clubs within ten miles of here. Models this size have to take off and land like full sized aircraft. You can't really fly any model aircraft from a boat. I am a professional seaman with a skipper's ticket but at the moment I'm taking time off to indulge myself flying, though at least half the pleasure is in the building and you can't make something as precise as this wing on a boat rolling about at sea.'

Jan handed him a mug of coffee and changed the subject. 'A couple of weeks ago Rose asked me to help her. I said I would be too busy.'

Paul smiled. 'So, I wasn't number one on her list.'

Jan laughed. 'Nor number two, she asked John Berry after me and I think it may have been him who mentioned you to her.'

'I've never met John Berry, but I suppose the chandlery grapevine has been working with its usual efficiency.'

'You won't have time to make two trips for us and take Rose to the Canaries unless the weather is perfect for you. And you can be quite sure that it won't be perfect for that length of time.'

'Yes, I know but I couldn't think of an excuse to reject the proposal right away, so I said I'd think about it and let her know in one week.'

Jan was looking at him, clearly needing to be convinced. Paul continued. 'Much as I'd love to sail a Choy Lee clipper, I have committed myself to doing the runs for you.'

'OK,' replied Jan.

Paul continued. 'I will however openly investigate the passage to the Canaries over the next couple of days. Part of my setting up red herrings tactic.'

'Red herrings?'

Paul started to explain what, in English, was meant by the expression but was interrupted by Jan. 'Yes, I know what it means but I ask myself why does he need to do this?'

The ease with which he and Jan had been conversing had led him to make the mistake of mentioning red herrings. 'Er, it keeps my options open,' he replied weakly.

Jan looked at him in silence for a moment then said. 'OK, now I understand where you are.'

Paul decided it was time to change the subject so asked Jan if he had a picture of what the model aircraft would look like when finished. He did and it was one of those old-fashioned high wing, single-piston-engined aircraft like the Lysander, a plane able to land and take off in fields. It was used to drop agents and their equipment behind enemy lines in World War Two. They discussed the Lysander's flying characteristics for a few minutes before shaking hands as Paul left.

On the way back to Sandpiper it occurred to him that he not only knew a criminal but also the criminal's hobby. And the same criminal now probably knew what he was planning for Ben. It also dawned that he was more comfortable in Jan's company than with any of his college colleagues, bar Anneke of course. And he'd got on pretty much instantly with Rose. Should he be with boating people rather than academic ones?

It was also obvious that in any rational thought process his college summer holiday was too short to fit in two 'runs' to Holland, one to the Canaries and a successful escape to wherever with Ben. The escape meant that he wasn't going back to the college of course but for it to be successful people had to believe he would return in September.

The perfect solution was staring him in the face - the delivery trip to the Canaries on the big, safe Choy Lee clipper would also be the escape. Audacity's crew could easily be taken for grandmother, son and grandson. Ben could be told that Rose liked to be called Nana. He and Ben could fly on to somewhere from the Canaries. A perfect solution except for the fact that Rose would have to be persuaded to play along with the plan and she was far too strong a character to do that. Being a mother herself she would almost certainly find out where Debbie lived and warn her. No, it was a great pity, but he'd have to decline Rose's invitation in one week, giving him time to openly research long sea passages in small boats.

His mind flickered back to Jan's plane, a big boy's toy. He idly supposed that model aircraft flying clubs were not overflowing with lady members. At this point his subconscious must have made a link with the idea of himself and Ben posing as Rose's family and thus unlikely to be noticed by those on the lookout for a man and a snatched small boy. They wouldn't be looking for a man and a small girl either. Suitably dressed, could Ben pass for a girl?

He knew that masquerading as the opposite sex formed the basis of many stories, most requiring considerable suspension of belief, but they may be in with a good chance of success with Ben. On a crude scale of small boy's facial features from mini thug at one end to sensitive or artistic at the other Ben was close to the sensitive end and his hair was already long, Debbie much preferring the artistic look for her son. And Ben didn't seem much interested in toy cars, train sets, water pistols and other 'boy' stuff, he just seemed to want to learn about the world.

If his latest idea had a chance of working, then he'd have to put time in seeing how (clothed!) small girls differed from small boys. Without hearing their name or hearing them speak how do you know which is which? If it was a matter of colour and style of clothing, then that would be easy to change. Hair probably wouldn't be a problem either. They could make a game of it - when aboard the boat they would play different people. Daddy, beard growing by the day, would play Terry or Harry (say) and Ben be a young girl called Cordelia or something similar. When Debbie first discovered she was pregnant they'd discussed names and swiftly homed in on Benjamin or Cordelia. So, Ben could temporarily be the Cory or Delia that he might have been. On second thoughts though ... Debbie knew this link to the name as well as he did so, on the off chance she might guess what was going on, he'd have to suggest another name to Ben. He'd always like ones ending in a - Vanessa, Emma, Virginia ... there were plenty to choose from. All in all, Ben passing for a girl for a short time may be a workable option. Things could be starting to turn his way.

Late Thursday morning, rather than cycling he caught the train back to the village, saving energy for the afternoon with Ben. Oddly, now that he knew he was in the last few weeks at college he put more thought and effort into teaching and surprised himself by enjoying it. Perverse, though of course he would not be able to keep it up. Was it possible to keep it up for a 30 to 40-year career? Was there a strategy or a method he could learn that made it bearable to teach year after year after year? Surely the long holidays on their own couldn't compensate for 20 to 30 hours a week of being the centre of attention in class, the one on whom action depends? Or did this come naturally to some people, they accepted that this is what they were? There must be a way of not burning yourself out, doing just enough to get exam passes for those who deserve them. And these successes plus the long holidays are what sees you through to your pension he presumed. But in an Index of Age at Death how did teachers compare with other professions? Clearly, he could do a Google search but what would be the point, there were so many factors, location being an obvious one. There must be some places where success is measured by how many of your class can you can keep off the streets for the afternoon; or where an hour's lesson does not result in a knifing. He's been lucky, most of his students were there because they wanted to be, they could see the long-term benefit of jumping through the necessary hoops. What right did he have to whinge about anything to do with the job, the secure future he's about to reject? What a fool, it was a job many would envy. A job he's leaving, there would be no secure pension for Paul Williams.

Doubts about his plans continued to grow until he realised that the train was about to pass the end of Davison's Dyke. He looked through the trees and was rewarded with a quick glimpse of Sandpiper and a longer lasting feeling of regret. He could not sell Sandpiper without arousing suspicion of course so he would have to just leave her there. Desert his home, his refuge. Leave her to gather grime and bills until the dyke owners' agent gained legal possession and sold her off cheaply to recover mooring fees. Yet another addition to eBay listings already rich with repossessed and project boats. It was a depressing thought.

Due to pick up Ben in an hour he tried to raise spirits by working through in his head what seemed to be a Debbie standard access schedule - a little Sandpiper time, a newly purchased ball to kick followed by a cycle ride to McDonald's for whatever was the least evil thing on the menu. Not looking forward to the food was pure prejudice since he'd never been in a McDonald's, but he had learned this week that the diner was neutral territory, the nation's favourite access day handover spot. He was going to be with his like.

The afternoon passed well enough. Ben seemed a little non-plussed at the change in emphasis but willing to play along. Towards the end of the afternoon Paul asked his son if he would like a day at the beach with his father? Yes! Ben was enthusiastic. A long train ride to the beach, yes please!

They arrived at Ben's home around 5 p.m. As before, MGBman's car was in the drive. As before, Debbie answered the door and Ben rushed past her into the house. Paul had steeled himself for this particular ending of access afternoon so was able to find a neutral voice to ask if, when the weather was suitable during the college summer holidays, he could pick Ben up at 9 a.m. for a day at the beach at Yarmouth or Lowestoft? By train of course.

Debbie looked at him in silence for a few seconds then said, 'I'll think it over and let you know.'

He thanked her and turned to go, happy that at least she didn't say no. Plan A was still on its feet.

Weeks ago, he'd arranged to visit his mother in London for the weekend so on Friday early evening he caught the train thinking that he would use the nearly two-hour journey time to review how things were going. On the plus side nothing appeared to be blocking progress and, although it's only been three sessions so far, he and Anneke had come to a quick and natural easiness in each other's company. He was looking forward to lunchtimes next week and had the impression she might be too. He'd read somewhere that the Dutch are the tallest race in Europe. Wearing her sensible flat shoes Anneke was only a couple of inches shorter than himself. She was not a conventional 'stunna' (the man opposite was reading a red-top) but with her long blonde hair, roundish face and upright stance she was very much of the classical Dutch mould. A proper woman. The word came to him then - wholesome. Yes, wholesomely attractive. It must be all that good food the Dutch are so adept at producing, he thought, then realised that the word wholesome could be taken as damning with faint praise. Anything but, she wore no make-up and didn't need to. There was nothing brittle about her. She was as nature intended and all the more attractive for it. A proper woman he found himself repeating.

He realised he was feeling happy and quickly fell into silly mode. If they started paying for their own sandwiches would they be Going Dutch? If their sessions took twice as long would the language be Double Dutch to him?

In her late fifties Jane Williams remained an attractive woman. Of medium height, slim, her brown hair cut in a short elfin style that emphasised her narrow high cheek-boned face. 'Welcome my big boy!' she said, looking upwards before hugging him tightly.

The last few days had changed his perspective. Walking into his mother's flat reminded him once more that she was herself an experienced escapologist. Once he was settled at university, she had left his stepfather and started life again in this one room plus kitchen and bathroom that she liked to describe as being in Holland Park, though an internet search indicated that it might be a street or three into Notting Hill Gate. Whatever, she appeared to be happy living what she said was her simple life. He thought once more how alike they were and wondered if he'd passed on this ... this what - hermit gene to Ben?

She was also something of a film buff and her DVD shelf had what was probably complete collections of films associated with Nicholas Roeg and Peter Greenaway. Other titles included Blade Runner, the final director's cut of course, not the original studio released version. He noticed that since his last visit she'd added three comparatively recent DVDs about the Donald Crowhurst story. He knew the name and had a vague idea of what had happened but no more.

On the next shelf lay a paperback of Kate Bush lyrics. A train ticket marked a page. *Oh England, my lionheart / dropped from my black Spitfire to my funeral barge* he read and was filled with a sudden and overwhelming love for his mother.

'We are so alike,' he shouted through to her in the kitchen.

It was a few seconds before she replied. 'I did grow you, you know.'

'I was looking through your DVDs and remembering how much I like most of them.'

'Choose one for us to watch after supper, which will be five minutes.'

He selected The Night of the Hunter, an ancient black and white film starring Robert Mitchum and Shelley Winters. It was a film of its period and thus dated in terms of dialogue and acting style, but he'd remembered two children escaping in a boat. He couldn't recall that sequence in detail but remembered being impressed.

The film was set in the poverty of dustbowl era USA. Two young children, a boy and a girl, are being hunted by the stepfather who had murdered their mother. Towards the end of the film they escape in a rowing boat being carried downriver by the current. There follows a dreamy sequence where the viewer sees in the background the children passing slowly left to right in their boat. In the foreground is a languorous succession of non-threatening creatures - rabbits, a turtle, a frog. No voiceover is necessary, the calm of the foreground creatures is mirrored by the children and their slow progress. Nature has accepted them. They will escape. In this part of the only film he ever directed, Charles Laughton had shown that it is possible to be both peaceful and purposeful. To Paul it was a brilliant minute or two of footage, almost painterly in its execution. If on canvas, a screenshot of the foreground rabbits and the background children would be talked of as a masterpiece.

His mother was looking at him as he repackaged the DVD. 'Escape in a boat?' she asked.

With his mind still on that dreamlike footage he answered. 'If only.'

'You are vulnerable at the moment. You need to think of the wider implications of any action,' she continued.

He tried to reassure her but the easy-going relaxed atmosphere of earlier in the evening had gone.

Early Saturday morning they drank a quick cup of coffee then walked for five minutes to reach the Portobello Road and its market. Most of his mother's sparse furniture had been sourced cheaply here. They browsed before the market was flooded with tourists and in late morning treated themselves to a spicy noodle brunch at one of the street food stalls.

The noodles and the rain which was about to set lengthily in made it obvious how the rest of the day should be spent - Blade Runners. The director's cut of the original film in the afternoon and the recently released sequel in the evening.

Both of them had seen the original a number of times but were, yet again, impressed by director Ridley Scott's bravery in allowing the film to be so apparently bleak. Dark and rainy Los Angeles was a horrible place to live in. Roy Batty's final realisation that his four-year android lifespan was superior to a human's much longer one (*I've seen things you people wouldn't believe* ...). And Scott makes you work for an understanding - you need to have picked up clues from the Latino detective (his little matchstick figures, his final words) to know that, right at the end, the Blade Runner's half smile when he sees a matchstick figure on the floor means that he and Rachel will successfully escape to the North. If any film bears repeat viewings, it's this one they agreed.

Paul had not seen the sequel, Blade Runner 49, before and was looking forward to comparing it. The film proved disappointing on first viewing despite good performances from Ryan Gosling and Harrison Ford plus some interesting ideas (Sinatra singing in a transparent bubble - *set 'em up Joe*). Overall though it was as if the studio had demanded a 50-50 mix of the original and a formulaic Bond film with its outrageously over the top baddies. In comparison it seemed rather dumbed down though more viewings might reveal some subtleties, though it's unlikely they agreed.

On Sunday morning he picked up the book of Kate Bush lyrics and opened it at his mother's bus ticket. 'England My Lionheart?' he asked her.

'Oh, it's just that I wanted to think the words through,' she replied.

'Why is the Spitfire coloured black?' he continued.

Her Paul. Her little technologist. Her boy who could discuss in depth things like the shape of the plane's wings. Typically, though, he'd picked up the odd colour of the plane while missing completely the point of the song. She said. 'Take it as a challenge. Have a few minutes then give me some possibilities of why it may be black.'

Paul smiled at his mother, recalling this challenging part of her character. Her frequent response to her young son's why, why questions. He thought for a few moments then said. 'I know Kate Bush has written some songs from the viewpoint of a woman's role in life. And I know that during World War 2 female pilots delivered newly made fighting aircraft from the factory to their allocated squadrons.

And I know that blackbirds fly low over open spaces to make it hard for predators like hawks to catch them. So, flying at low altitude a matt black plane may be more difficult for an enemy pilot to see ...' He came to a halt, the more he said about this possibility the less likely it seemed.

'Yes, I'm aware that women did make those flights in the war,' said his mother. 'But there may be a clue in the next line. Perhaps it's a Spitfire because the plane is a British icon and it's black to connect it to the funeral barge of the next line. Connection of the comparatively modern icon of the Spitfire to the ancient one of a funeral barge may represent the passage of time. Perhaps the whole song is a dying person's homage to their country and its history. The person is seeing flickering images that to him or her represent this country - the bridge in the rain, ravens in the tower. English icons. I'm not certain about any of this of course. It's bookmarked so I can put more time into it.'

He quickly scanned the song's words and structure. 'You're right, yet again. It's written from the viewpoint of someone dying or, alternatively, having to leave the country. I don't want to go is repeated.' He was silent for a moment then added, 'I just hope your qualities have found their way to Ben.'

'We are unable to choose which parts of us we pass on. Philip Larkin got it all right with *This be the*

Verse,' she replied.

Paul knew how lucky he was that he and his mother could have this sort of exchange. No need for the posturing, the defensive manoeuvres and the point scoring that often colour colleague discussions. How sad it was that their family was so fragmented, Ben's paternal grandmother would be so good for him. And vice versa perhaps, though his mother seemed to have found a way of keeping her losses, her regrets, in a compartment that she could remove herself from, for most of the time, leaving behind the grief her losses carry. Compartment - The Hurt Locker he suddenly thought, another cinematic reference.

Wanting to continue the discussion, he said, 'When Glen Campbell died recently Wichita Lineman got a lot of airtime. I looked up the song's words. A hardworking, resourceful man goes about his job. In the background there is a longing for someone from his past and he could do with a vacation. But he continues to work, a role model of the self-sufficient, honest man. And I realised that this experienced and effective working man image has been a well-used one - the Marlbro cowboy, the Mitsubishi pick up man you don't mess with and do you remember the year of my two winters?'

She replied with a smile. Twenty years ago, at the start of the school summer holiday, she'd put her 15-year-old son on a flight to Melbourne to spend a few weeks of the Australian winter helping her brother Ted expand buildings on his sheep farm. It wasn't that Ted had been in need of help it was more that she wanted to expose Paul to her brother's work ethic and his toughness. It had been a success she thought.

He continued. 'There was a beer advert on television that was a classic. Picture this ... An outback farm. It's hot. The apprentice has mucked up a vital machine, again. Cue appearance of grizzled mechanic. Machine fixed. The ad ends with the grizzled mechanic putting an ice-cold glass of beer to his lips as the voiceover says, '*when you've had a real bludge of a day, Cairns Bitter eh,*' Paul said the last bit with a cod Oz accent.

His mother laughed, 'I certainly do remember, you were using the word bludge for months afterwards.' There's hope for her son yet she thought, then had a second thought - adverts for beer, cigarettes and pick-up trucks. Men.

He pointed to the three Crowhurst DVDs. 'These are new since my last visit, have you become interested in sailing?' he asked.

'Not as such but, as you know, I admire the work of Nicholas Roeg. I read somewhere that, years ago now, he asked permission from Clare Crowhurst to film the story. She refused then but has allowed films to be made recently, due to the 50th anniversary of the Golden Globe race I assume. Or is some copyright law involved? I don't know but watching The Mercy is a wonderful excuse to ogle Colin Firth.'

'Somebody once foolishly mentioned that I look a bit like Colin Firth.'

She smiled, 'A bit perhaps,' then added, 'I almost forgot to mention that there's a small link to you, beyond the obvious sailing one.'

His raised eyebrows invited her to continue. 'Crowhurst's plywood trimaran was made as a bare shell in Brightlingsea and fitted out in your village.'

Surprised he asked, 'Can you remember the name of the village boatyard?'

'No, sorry.'

'It doesn't matter, most of the boatyards have gone now having turned into small marinas making their money only from moorings. But they are all less than a mile from Sandpiper's mooring. I'll have to immerse myself in the story. Can I borrow the DVDs? I'll get myself a small 12-volt player and post them back to you in two weeks.'

'Take them with you. I suggest you view them in the order Deep Water followed by The Mercy and then finally Crowhurst. Deep Water sets out the story of the Golden Globe and the larger than life characters who started the race. When viewing The Mercy pay attention to the speech of Clare Crowhurst (Rachel Weisz) when she addresses the throng of reporters. It's right at the end of the film and it's as appropriate today as it was fifty years ago. Nicholas Roeg himself was one of the producers of Crowhurst. It has a much more adventurous structure, as you might expect.'

He had done no preparation for teaching in the coming week so caught an early train back to East Anglia. He had to have easily explained answers to another two or three exam questions for the accountants' class at 9 a.m. tomorrow. Had he enjoyed a weekend with his mother living what passed for a normal life or had it been a weekend of what was largely make believe, indulging themselves in the imagined world of films and song lyrics?

It was more likely to be the latter he thought. He'd managed to put his situation behind him for two days and (just) held it together when saying goodbye to his mother feeling that, at worst, he may never see her again. She had known something was afoot and made him promise to talk over any big decisions (her term) with her beforehand. She is so astute he found himself thinking. The films we viewed featured vulnerable people escaping. Could she possibly home in on his real situation?

On the train he quickly succumbed to depression, telling lies of this magnitude to his mother did not come naturally. And yet here he was, a criminal in the making, a person who from now on would not be able to avoid deceiving others. A loathsome bastard, wholly unworthy of the love of his mother and Ben. A person who should not be presenting himself to Anneke as a man planning an innocent cruise to her homeland. He tried to lighten things by searching for mild ways of describing his current mental state, *I am a person of low self-esteem,* for example. Unsurprisingly, it didn't work.

On Monday he was not feeling so bad about himself. At College the accounting class was fully attended and went well enough and the lunch session with Anneke was enjoyable. They both explained, mostly in English, what they'd done at the weekend. Inspired by Paul's boating interests, Anneke had walked part of the Wherryman's Way, the path beside the Yare used by sailors going to their boats a century ago. She'd seen the Norfolk Broads at its best and its worst, from a beautifully varnished traditional yacht tacking silently and efficiently upriver to a hirecruiser with tinnie clutching louts cavorting on the roof, heavy metal booming from below. The latter had not put her off and they agreed to take Sandpiper for a sail on the following Sunday.

Feeling apprehensive about the performance expected of him later in the evening he arrived at the coffee house fifteen minutes early and sat close to the door with a clear view outside. It was then that he realised he didn't know what sort of car Emma had. What was the opposite of an experienced lothario? An inexperienced one he supposed, or, for an even shorter answer, me. If the car had tinted windows how would he know that it's her? Christ, he'd give anything to be cycling back to Sandpiper with the most pressing thing on his mind being what to cook for himself. He was certainly suffering from self-inflicted complications.

A silver Ford Ka, not the latest model, stopped outside. Recognising Emma he quickly left the cafe, opened the passenger door and got in expecting an immediate tyre squealing drive away from the kerb. In reality they had to wait in full view of the passing world for half a minute before a break in the traffic allowed them to pull out.

'I should have brought my Bill Clinton mask,' he said in an attempt to relieve his tension.

'I'm glad you didn't, I'd be fighting off middle aged women by the hundreds,' Emma replied, seeming to be astonishingly calm and controlled in comparison to his jittery self. 'Remember that you're off to meet my husband to talk about sailing so calm and chatty is the look of the moment,' she added, briefly looking across and smiling at him.

'I still find it incredible that you've sat quietly in class for the whole academic year and are now calmly whisking me off to have your way with me.'

She frowned, 'I don't want to put pressure on you, Paul. Let's just enjoy being together, finding out about each other. The earth isn't going to shatter, I just want to be part of your life while it's possible. See how you live, talk frankly to you.'

He unclipped his seat belt, leaned over and kissed her thigh through her jeans. 'Point taken, Miss Delicious.'

They parked at the top of the lane and walked down over the railway line to the dyke, Emma carrying a small shopping bag with, he assumed, everything she needed in it. In the warm early evening the place seemed to be on its best behaviour - the pathway was dry, a pair of swans were gliding along nearby and the drone of diesel engines passing at the far end of the dyke was barely audible.

'So, home sweet home,' he said as they stopped at Sandpiper's gangplank.

Emma was smiling broadly. 'This is lovely, and romantic, I'm so glad to be here with you.' She put down her bag, took his head in both hands and kissed him on the lips, letting it last long enough to be taken as intimacy rather than joyful, friendly kiss.

'I needed that,' he said, simply and honestly, putting his arms around her.

'And I've wanted to do it for a long time,' she

replied, her arms over his shoulders.

They remained closely bound, becoming gradually accustomed to the other's feel, their relative size and the growing sense that their encounter had a legitimacy, a harmony, a bond. He kissed her forehead. 'I think it is time to show Madame her penthouse suite. The unliveried flunky will carry her bag.'

'Shouldn't he be carrying Madame instead?' she asked then, having noticed the tripping hazards that were Sandpiper's stanchions and guard wires, she added. 'No, make it the bag.'

Inside the cabin he avoided boating terms and introduced her to the larder/kitchen/dining room/lounge (all eight feet by eight of it), the toilet in which it was just possible to turn around (if careful) and the bedroom (seven feet wide at the head end, two at the foot and no floor at all, it being necessary to climb into bed from the central walkway).

He had been afraid she'd be horrified at the boat's small size and well used condition, but her face showed pleasure. 'This is really cute, when you next stand in front of the class I'll know exactly where you come from. And I'll know what it's like to have been close to you.'

He'd bought a bottle of red wine, Carmenere, and they sat in the warm cockpit drinking it. Paul noticed that she was taking small sips. 'The wine not to your taste?' he asked.

'It's not that, I'm taking it easy because thought we'd have to drive to a pub to eat.'

'Certainly not. Sandpiper rule number one states that on the first night the skipper must be the chef for the crew, though it will be simple fare cooked on two gas rings.'

'In that case I'll tuck into the wine. Have many previous guests enjoyed the privilege of being wined, dined and whatevered here?'

He tried to think of some jaunty sort of response and failed. 'The honest answer is that you are the first for all three activities, thus my nervousness.'

She put down her glass, leaned over and kissed him, more softly this time. 'I am honoured, you are a lovely man.'

'But not that careful a man, I forgot to ask if you are vegetarian, vegan, fruitarian, or only eat chargrilled fennel, or ...'

'Omnivore. Cook me what you will.' She finished her wine and refused a refill saying she'd take a walk to view the neighbouring boats while he cooked their supper.

He put the kettle on to boil and placed an Oxo cube ready in a bowl. He chopped carrots and celery into fat matchsticks and an onion into fine slivers, putting them into the large pan to gently simmer in a little oil. Pouring boiling water into the bowl he broke up the Oxo cube, shook in some mixed herbs from a pot and added two handfuls of textured vegetable protein (tvp) chunks. He put on another full kettle to boil and opened a packet of wholewheat fusilli ready to be cooked in the smaller pan. The tvp chunks quickly softened having absorbed most of the bowl's liquid so he added them to the simmering vegetables. By this time Emma had returned, refilled her glass and was sitting in the cockpit watching him with an amused expression. 'I thought you were just going to open a couple of cans,' she said.

'When you taste this you'll probably wish I had,' he responded, adding snap peas into the pasta for its final four minutes of cooking time. When done he drained the pasta and peas and added them to the large pan, mixing everything together. He relocated the small cabin table to the cockpit and passed out two forks plus two pieces of kitchen roll. 'Never let it be said that I don't know how to treat a girl, no expense spared.'

'It will never be said.' She raised her glass 'And here's to my tutor, my chef and my lover.'

Paul raised his glass in return. 'Regarding the latter, you do realise, or you're about to, that I am long out of practice?'

'Two things. Firstly, I'm going to enjoy providing you with the practice. Secondly, I will be more than content for us to lie naked with each other, talking openly and frankly, learning about each other. I've known you for eight months now and what I most want is closeness and tenderness from a man I admire. Speech over, let's eat,' she added before he could say more, though what he would have found to say he didn't know.

Emma quickly realised that the 'meat' was tvp but the meal proved good enough to end with two clean plates. They continued to sit in the cockpit, slowly finishing the wine and exchanging greetings with old Jimmy as he checked on his boat further down the dyke. Eventually Paul said, 'Bedtime?'

'I'll stay here while you go first then you can watch me get ready,' she said.

'You'll miss seeing me putting on my Rupert Bear pyjamas,' he warned, trying to relieve his the-moment-is-coming tension.

She laughed. 'Best to avoid the Rupert Bears. And don't be anxious, enjoy!'

Naked he lay on his front in the centre of the forecabin berth watching her slowly undress down to lacy black bra and pants. He had an erection, thank heavens. Her slim figure had not one gram of excess. 'You are absolutely gorgeous. During the last couple of classes, I've been seeing just a hint of your nipples and loving it. Now I know why.'

'Then you saw exactly what you were meant to see,' she said as she kneeled and pulled his head to her breasts, their nipples erect. He kissed them through the thin material then kissed the bare flesh as she took her bra off. A few moments later she stood and pulled his head to her pants which were sufficiently sheer to just see her pubic triangle. Kissing her there he thought he could sense a faint whiff of vaginal juices or perhaps it was no more than a hint of a remembered from long ago smell.

She stepped out of her pants, slipped past him onto the bed and straddled him as he turned over. She guided him in then bent to kiss him on the lips, her hair hanging down onto and past his face leaving him with the feeling he'd been captured. A most willing prisoner.

She started rocking back and forth as he slowly ran his hands over her hips and thighs. It had been so long since he had felt the smooth skin of a young woman, too long. As feared, he came far too early and started to apologise but she put a finger on his lips and moved forward to be almost above his head. He bent his legs and moved down the berth to be directly below her, looking up at pubic hair glistening with her juices and basking in their glorious smell. He started kissing and licking before probing with his tongue for the place which would bring her an orgasm. He heard her say, 'mm, yes,' and worked there with his tongue, slowly at first until she gave a cry and moved back far enough to look down at him and smile. 'Thank you.'

They held this position for a few moments, smiling to each other until she said, 'I want to be close to you not myself so, my lover, you will need to wash your face.'

'I was hoping to be able to smell you for weeks but, since you ask so nicely, I'll introduce you to Sandpiper's sophisticated ablution facilities, aka the larger of the two plastic bowls in this cupboard. Let the ship's log hereby record that I am willing to invest in another so we can have matching his 'n her bowls should madame insist on having her own facility in the future.'

'A madame prepared to mix and match bodily fluids is quite prepared to share a plastic bowl, the same water even, if necessary.'

Later they lay together in the forecabin talking and touching. She insisted on hearing his life story tonight - all of it, she said - and promised to tell him hers the next time they were here.

In the morning he gained consciousness to find Emma holding his erect penis, looking into his eyes, smiling and saying, 'Hello and welcome to the world where a student holds her teacher's todger.'

He couldn't immediately think of anything to say but, luckily, didn't need to as she continued. 'I was interested in seeing how long it takes to grope someone awake, found you nearby and went for it.'

'How long did it take?'

'One minute seventeen.'

'I've obviously infected you with WSH, Williams Sense of Humour, a disease for which there is no known cure.'

'I'm pleased about that, it's one of the many odd features that make you attractive to me.'

'The honourable member for Davison's Dyke North is most grateful for the attraction.'

'And a fine upstanding member he is too, lucky constituents.'

She showed no sign of letting go so he had to ask, 'And in size comparison with the mean and standard deviation of all UK males?'

'In the upper quartile I believe but the sample size is still quite small.'

'How small?'

'In my new Wicked Seducer phase it's currently one. But what a one!' she cried, smothered his face with kisses then quickly got out of the berth before he could return fire.

'Argh,' she exclaimed a moment later. 'We've got to get a move on. It's almost eight and there's Cost Accounting revision at nine. On the class bucket list, it's second only to watching paint dry. I've got to be there.'

Driving into the city they agreed to be more discreet in future by making their own way to

Sandpiper. Now she knew the number of the boat's combination lock she could make herself at home while he travelled back by bike and train.

FIVE

2019

He started researching potential safe havens for himself and Ben. This couldn't be done in isolation - having decided that they'd get to this safe haven in a small yacht then it was also necessary to investigate the weather patterns they were likely to meet on the way. But finding a safe haven came first.

Since he was openly studying Dutch, it made sense to find out which other countries spoke that language. There were more than he first thought. Suriname on the northeast coast of South America and, more usefully perhaps, the ABC islands off the northern coast of Venezuela. The former Dutch colonies of Aruba, Bonaire and Curacao each had a number of harbours on their leeward side and they were likely to have a fair number of foreign flagged yachts so he and Ben would not stand out. Using the Gunton supplied phone on a pay as you go sim card, he researched each potential haven, flitting between Wikipaedia's summary statistics, harbours and possible hazards on Navionics, and average annual weather data on Weatherspark. To his surprise he also discovered that English was the official language in Guyana, Suriname's neighbour to the immediate west. The only country in South America where English is spoken widely. Unfortunately, a few minutes more searching revealed that this former British colony was rated a poor country with a high level of street crime. But there was a note that plentiful oil reserves had been recently discovered offshore. His first thought was good, his second thought was that the oil would just increase the gap between rich and poor, leading to yet more crime. No matter how financially stressed he and Ben were, on the street they would probably appear rich whities, aka fair game. There would be teaching opportunities though ... there was no point in going into great detail at this point, he realised, it was enough to know that they had options.

Getting to the Caribbean or South America would involve an Atlantic crossing of course. They would need a strong, seaworthy yacht and finances dictated that it would have to be a small one. So be it.

In the city library's sailing section, he found Jimmy Cornell's World Cruising Routes and World Cruising Handbook. They were old 1990 editions but proved a mine of information on weather systems for long distance sailors. To avoid the hurricane season in the Caribbean the usual advice for those crossing the Atlantic from Europe is to leave the Canaries no earlier than mid-November and follow the route pioneered by Christopher Columbus over 500 years earlier. That is head south west until just north of the Cape Verde Islands then west on the approximate latitude of your destination. This takes advantage of the favourable tradewinds and ocean currents in these latitudes. Voyagers starting a little later, say around Christmas, are likely to find more consistent winds but the longer the advantageous wind and current persists the higher the seas heap up in the Caribbean where it can be very rough indeed in the west by March. They'd be in a small yacht so it was clear to Paul that it would be an early start for them. Being just off the north coast of Venezuela, the ABC islands were said to be below the hurricane belt, but not by much. To play safe they'd follow the usual crossing advice, he decided. Also, to minimise the likelihood of bad weather, World Cruising Routes advised northern Europeans to be south of the Bay of Biscay by mid-September. So, Paul noted, we need to be away by the end of August.

There are very few publications for voyagers travelling long distances in small boats, so everybody absorbs much the same information resulting in the Portuguese islands of Madeira and the Spanish Canaries (particularly the latter) becoming crowded with yachts waiting for the Atlantic crossing weather window. More internet research left Paul with the impression that Spanish officials were the least likely to be fussy about entry formalities. Maybe a non-stop passage from Portsmouth to the Canaries was the best plan? When approaching the Canaries then head for somewhere likely to be packed with other potential Atlantic crossers, say Los Christianos on Tenerife or one of the smaller islands, Gomera perhaps?

Portsmouth to Los Christianos was a long way though. Paul extended the area coverage of the Gunton supplied charting package and started planning in more detail. It was around 1600 nautical miles to Los Christianos assuming a straightforward passage, but it could be as much as a thousand more if they had to battle headwinds for some of the way. A hell of an introduction to sailing for a small boy. It could take 16 days or a month, possibly more, to make the passage. Whatever boat he'd bought in Portsmouth would have to be stocked with at least five weeks' worth of tinned and packet food. If they left Portsmouth near the end of August then they'd be waiting in the Canaries (hiding in plain sight, he hoped) for around a couple of months before tackling the Atlantic. Playing the weather windows, they ought to be in the ABC islands by Christmas, four months and almost 5000 nautical miles after leaving Portsmouth. A missing boy should not be big news on the other side of the Atlantic by then, he thought, and his passport was unlikely to be checked against a wanted list issued by the UK, assuming that they even received a list that far away. 'Portsmouth to Tenerife to the ABC islands,' he said under his breath. Seven easy words. Two long passages.

'Red herring time,' Paul said to the rest of the unoccupied dyke on Wednesday morning. It would dawn quickly on Debbie that he had snatched Ben, so it was necessary to confuse things with numerous false trails. He could use the college computer for whatever he liked but had to sign in and out. So, he researched what might seem to be relevant stuff on the traceable college system and did what was actually relevant on his phone or at a terminal in the city library. He worked up other actions that might add confusion. He put it about at college that he had applied for a fairly lowly research post at the University of Delft. That tied in nicely with the common room language sessions with Anneke and it would take Delft some time going around different departments to discover that they didn't have a research post advertised. Or if they did then it would take even longer to find that Paul hadn't applied for it. Right at the end, when he knew the snatch date, he'd book and pay for a cheap man and child flight to somewhere, anywhere as long as it was cheap, for two days after the snatch date so that while police waited to arrest him at the airport they'd be to all intents and purposes invisible, over 100 miles from Portsmouth and aiming for the Atlantic. *Bootiful*, as Norfolk turkey magnate Bernard Mathews used to say.

On the college computer, since there was no point in disguising the fact that a snatch had been planned, he searched newspaper archives for stories about stolen or missing children. Were there common features in successful snatches? He had the sort of mind that asked how one would measure success in this context? Never found perhaps? He knew the words snatch and success shouldn't be in the same sentence but managed to quell his unease by concentrating on the challenge. Many cases in the archives seemed to involve different nationalities of the parents so there was another family in another country to go to. In this case the snatcher had people on his side but that's not an advantage he would have. Other cases were a complete mystery, an attractive child just disappeared without trace. He did other obvious searches, seeking which countries did not have an extradition treaty with the UK then assessing them in terms of language, cost of living, life expectancy, crime ... it soon became clear that a lack of an extradition treaty typically meant an unsafe place to be. No, not for them but anyone tracing his searches would find a confusion of clues.

On Wednesday afternoon he phoned Rose Bailey and said sorry but, with other things to which he's already committed, he couldn't find a slot which would allow plenty of time for bad weather. With relief he learned that a suitable person was waiting in the wings having contacted Rose a couple of days ago. She had said yes to the new man but only if Paul declined. They wished each other Bon Voyage.

That evening, lying naked face to face in the forecabin he reminded Emma that it was her turn with the life story. She was from an old Norfolk family living mostly in coastal villages north of Great Yarmouth. Fishing folk, farmers. One of her great uncles was Charlie Rigg, a celebrated lifeboatman who'd earned several decorations for saving those in peril on the sea - she amused and charmed him by singing those last few words, as if in church.

She'd fallen for a boy while in her final year at school and married him aged seventeen. They'd grown apart and eventually divorced. It had not been long before she met and married her current husband. During a bad night two years ago, she'd had a vision of herself in her forties, dissatisfied and angry as her fifth marriage turned sour. By the end of that night she'd resolved to dedicate herself to becoming a career professional. No more marriage. She would seek lovers when it seemed both appropriate and possible. And here she was.

'Am I the first?'

'You are and I have never made a better decision,'

she said, wrapping her arms and legs tightly around him then noisily kissing every bit she could reach from that close position. Almost eating me, he thought, surrendering happily to the sensation.

Debbie standard access day behaviour continued. The 'proper' father took his child to McDonald's. Their kick-a-ball session confirmed that Ben was no more likely than his father to be the next Harry Kane. They still had some time on Sandpiper but with less stress on developing Ben's mini engineer status. Paul started to take careful note of Ben's clothes size when the opportunity occurred. He delivered Ben back to Debbie and asked if she'd decided about their beach day.

'Yes, if the weather is suitable. Ring me on the day before and we'll make arrangements.' Trying not to show his joy, he nodded agreement and left. Plan A was still alive.

A few days ago he'd assumed that the weekend with his mother may be their last together, but he'd enjoyed it and thought that she had too. It couldn't be the last. Perhaps he could find a way of talking over his situation with her. As soon as that thought occurred, he knew how impossible it would be. *'Sorry Mum, but I'm going to snatch Ben and sail off to a destination neither you nor anyone else will ever know. You are about to lose your two nearest and dearest. Oh, and I'll do a drugs run to get the money. Is there any more tea in the pot?*

Utter stupidity. Nevertheless, he wanted one more weekend with his mother, so he not only viewed her Donald Crowhurst DVDs but also attempted a 1500 word summary of their story...

By today's standards the Sunday Times sponsored non-stop singlehanded around the world race for yachts in 1968 (the Golden Globe) was an oddity. Odd in the sense that the lone sailor could start any time between June 1st and October 31st. There were to be two awards - the first, the Golden Globe Trophy for the first sailor to return to the port they departed from and the second, £5000 for the fastest non-stop passage around the world. Stopping or receiving any form of help incurred automatic disqualification.

There were nine eventual starters, all male. Robin Knox-Johnson was the first away in early June. He was in the strong but comparatively slow yacht, Suhali. Construction had barely started on Crowhurst's trimaran when Suhali set off and it wasn't until October 31st, the last day for a valid departure, that his yacht made her ill-prepared leaving. She was now named Teignmouth Electron due to sponsorship from the Devon town. Her delivery trip from the Norfolk Broads to Teignmouth demonstrated that his boat was a poor performer under sail, well below Crowhurst's initial high hopes for a trimaran, a type of boat he'd never sailed before. Deep Water showed footage of the last couple of days before departure and Paul found it difficult viewing, the stress clearly showing on this man who knew then that he would not succeed but found himself unable to avoid the challenge. If he had withdrawn from the race, then it would have been disastrous in terms of their family finances and reputation but at least he and Claire and their four children would be together. It would be difficult, but they could rebuild their lives elsewhere. Crowhurst could not bring himself to withdraw and so started the race.

Many of the other starters were not well prepared either and by the time that Teignmouth Electron reached the equator there were only three other sailors left in the race - Robin Knox-Johnson in Suhali, Bernard Moitessier in Joshua and Nigel Tetley in Victress. The latter was a trimaran of the same class as Teignmouth Electron but a well sorted one that Tetley and his wife had been living on. All three were sailors with much more experience than Crowhurst - Knox-Johnson was a merchant navy officer, Tetley a Royal Navy officer and the charismatic Frenchman Moitessier a philosopher/yachtsman with many thousands of sea miles under his keel. There was no hope of Crowhurst catching up, nor could he prevent sea water entering his badly underspecified boat but by the time Teignmouth Electron was in the South Atlantic, off Argentina, he'd hatched a survival plan.

He'd go ashore at some remote place and get enough plywood to staunch the worst of the leaks. There was no hope whatsoever that his boat would survive the Southern Ocean and Cape Horn so instead he'd stay offshore in this area for some months before following the other three back towards home. Coming fourth and last would, he hoped, give him a chance to, somehow, save the family home and some face. There would be no prize, but he'd get credit for battling hard and bringing his ship back. For the plan to work he needed to be able to report at intervals false (but credible) 'positions' to his agent/publicist ashore in Teignmouth.

Nowadays sailors in around the world race know where they are to within a couple of metres and transmitters on their yachts tell race organisers where each competitor is. Fifty years ago, there was none of this so, to estimate their position sailors had to use a sextant to measure angles between the horizon and the sun, moon or stars. These were compared with published astronomical tables carried aboard and the workings entered into the ship's log. An experienced astronavigator could later check that a voyage had been completed by verifying a sample of the workings. Crowhurst devised a method of putting a dot on the chart then finding data from the published tables which matched his 'position' dot. He then entered his reverse engineered workings into the ship's log in their normal sequence. The race prize winners would certainly have their logs closely scrutinised but, Crowhurst thought, they were unlikely to check the last place man.

Sailors in a similar race today use satellites to send video clips of whatever they like. Fifty years ago at sea there were no long distance communication methods beyond ham radio. To speak to their family at home, report their estimated position to their agent or get news of their competitors a sailor's radio had to be patched through whichever shorebased radio station could be reached. This was not always easy, particularly for Crowhurst whose radio proved as unsuitable as his boat. He often had to spend hours tinkering with it so it was at infrequent intervals (and in rather vague language) that he reported his 'position' to his agent in Teignmouth who, as an ex Fleet Street man, knew how to add what might be called enhancement. Thus, everyone thought that Crowhurst was storming along and catching the others.

But fate was to deal Crowhurst's plan two blows from which there was no recovery. The first came when Moitessier who (despite sailing rapidly towards home and being the almost certain winner of the fastest passage prize) decided that it was senseless to continue North in search of awards. It was not in his soul. He turned and headed back to the Pacific, in effect sailing non-stop one and a half times around the world to Tahiti, where he subsequently spent many happy years. Moitessier followers have found that this behaviour was not unusual for him.

By now Robin Knox-Johnson had reached home to a well-deserved hero's welcome. The prize for the first man home was his but Nigel Tetley in Victress and (apparently) Donald Crowhurst in Teignmouth Electron were still in the race for the fastest non-stop circumnavigation.

The second and fatal blow to Crowhurst's plan came some days later. Reports of Crowhurst's 'rapid progress' were being relayed to Nigel Tetley who pushed Victress harder and harder, trying to beat this man who seemed, report after report, to be catching him and, even worse, doing so in the same class of boat. Victress was eventually pushed too hard and she started to break up, just 1100 miles from home. Tetley sent out a Mayday and was rescued.

Hearing this news, alone and disorientated in the ocean, Crowhurst was left with nowhere to go. To the waiting world he was now the sole remaining competitor and racing towards a hero's welcome in Teignmouth. Over the radio his publicist/agent told him of the town's excitement - *Teignmouth Welcomes Donald* banners were being made. But of course, if he arrived home as the only other finisher then his ship's log would be closely scrutinised and quickly exposed as fraudulent. He would be branded a liar and a cheat. His false reports had been the direct cause of Nigel Tetley's misfortune. He was going to be slaughtered by the press he had duped. The Crowhurst family would be homeless. His children would have to live with the stigma. It was unbearable. Teignmouth Electron's log showed that his mind was becoming increasingly disordered. In his last few days he imagined he had been playing a game against some Deity. A game he had lost. In July 1969 a British cargo boat found Teignmouth Electron drifting, abandoned. Her papers were in order. 'It is the mercy,' was one of the last entries in the log. The only possible conclusion was that he stepped off his boat into the sea, the deep water he had been in almost from the start...

To Paul, the writing of this summary brought home the fact that his current position was little better than that of Donald Crowhurst, a man condemned by his inexperience, his mistakes and some appallingly bad luck. None of us start experienced and everyone of us makes mistakes, Paul reasoned. We usually get away lightly with them but, now and again, the worst outcome must occur. He also realised that he'd developed deep sympathy and respect for Crowhurst, a fellow man whose internal world provided an escape route from the unbearable.

'He risked everything and failed, and there goes every one of us who dares to set off into the unknown,' Paul found himself saying, portentously. 'We don't know how we will react when things go drastically wrong.' He then remembered the end of that famous Donald Rumsfeld quotation - how right he was. It is not possible to be prepared against the unknown unknowns.

Pursuing the Ben dressed as a girl theme, Paul cycled to Pearson Gardens, a large park in the city's western suburbs. It had good walks, an extensive play area, a cafe and a boating lake. Most importantly, the cafe was next to the play area so he could sit at an outside table and try to answer the question of how do small girls differ from small boys when dressed for outdoors.

Observing without arousing suspicion that he was some sort of paedophile or pervert proved something of a trial. How was he supposed to make himself look innocent? By being innocent presumably, but how did he get that appearance? The more he thought about how others might view him the more anxious he became. Sitting there it swiftly became clear that he was unsuited to a late career as a private detective - he didn't even have a proper name for a start. No, the incomes of Cormoran Strike, Jackson Brodie and their like were unlikely to be under threat from plain Paul Williams. In the end he pretended to be a parent and so looked directly at the play area wearing what he hoped was a benign expression. Nobody challenged him and he soon came to the conclusion that in a pink top, blue jeans and pink shoes Ben would easily pass for a Cordelia, a Vanessa or a Whoeva. The idea was a goer.

On Sunday Anneke caught the train and Paul met her at the station. With no planning whatsoever they kissed on the lips, drew back and smiled at each other.

'What happened to the air kiss on both cheeks phase?' she asked him, teasingly.

'As long as it's a short phase I'll go through that foreign gesture stuff if you insist on it,' he replied, pretending distaste.

'I am happy as we are,' she said, taking his arm. 'Now whisk me off to your yacht and impress me with your great wealth.'

'As you will see, Sandpiper and wealth don't go well together,' he replied, delighted at their easy rapport. The close and slightly jokey relationship which had developed quickly on the neutral territory of the college was clearly continuing in what he supposed an outsider might regard as more his home ground than hers.

Both the weather and the tides were perfect for a sail downriver then back part way to anchor in Eastland Broad for a late lunch. After which she insisted on washing up and, sitting in the cockpit, he shot quick glances at her standing in the galley, sleeveless top and shorts emphasising her lean, athletic build. The desire to lick her lightly tanned thighs was almost overwhelming.

'I can feel your eyes,' she said, half smiling but not looking at him.

No, you could feel my tongue he thought, but said, 'I was thinking how lucky I am that such an attractive, interesting and intelligent woman had agreed to come on the boat today.'

'I can't live up to that.'

'Au contraire, it was a pre-requisite of the invitation.'

'We are supposed to be studying Dutch not French,' she said, accepting his lightening of the tone.

Later, saying their 'Tot Ziens' after a lingering kiss at the station she said that she hoped they would go for a longer sail, a two- or three-day cruise perhaps, on the Markermeer during the summer holidays.

The invitation to become lovers perhaps? 'You won't be able to keep me away,' he assured her.

Thoughts about what Sandpiper may contain by the time they sailed together in Holland put a damper on things as he walked back to the dyke. The remedy was obvious though, they'd have to have their mini cruise before the 'consignment' was stowed aboard. He was not going to infect her with his criminality.

Beach day! Man and boy cycled to the village station and caught the 0925 for Lowestoft. The train was not crowded and Ben, more accustomed to travelling while strapped into a car seat, was excited by the fact that he could move from one side of the train to the other, unfettered viewing. One consequence of Norfolk being such a flat county is that few parts are much above sea level. Railway tracks here are certainly not much above so you get the unique Broads scene of a distant gaff rigged yacht appearing to glide over fields. In fact, the yacht is in a narrow river but you can't see the water, so it looks as if the locals have developed a sport called cross country sailing. Yes, here we *do diffrent*.

At low speed they crossed the river on the swing bridge at Reedham then travelled south parallel to the New Cut seeing mostly motorboats taking the short cut between the rivers Yare and Waveney. At Somerleyton they crossed the Waveney on their second swing bridge of the day and watched a yacht sailing downriver towards the bridge.

'Will the bridge open for the yacht, Daddy?'

'Yes, but not yet. The yacht will have to sail around in front of the bridge for a few minutes before the bridgekeeper can open it.' Paul demonstrated a ninety-degree horizontal swing with his arm. Ben replicated the arm movement a few times while his father wondered if he should introduce the idea of thermal expansion and contraction - for the last few years these metal swing bridges, designed and constructed in the Edwardian era, had been unable to open during those occasional extremely hot summer days that the country had been enjoying. On those days bridgekeepers were sometimes able to offer a late evening opening when the metal had cooled and contracted enough to be sure that it would close again with the tracks aligned properly. Railtrack usually played it safe though, a bridge unable to close for a few hours would cause a great deal of havoc for the travelling public. Better to disgruntle a few yachties who'd have to hassle their masts down then up again to continue their sailing. Paul smiled, miffed yachties, probably not the worst outcome of global warming. Unless you're one of them of course.

At Lowestoft they headed for the south beach buying the necessary bucket and spade on the way. Ben showed interest in the boats in the Royal Norfolk & Suffolk Yacht Club basin, mostly yachts but also the RNLI lifeboat and one or two other interesting looking craft at the eastern end of the basin. They agreed to come back an hour early to investigate this part of the harbour thoroughly.

They soon got into beach mode, building a sandcastle near the water so that a moat could be excavated. Building, paddling ... beach activities continued until lunchtime when they went to a cafe for fish and chips. Some kind soul had demolished their sandcastle by the time they returned to their former spot on the beach. Paul was surprised and pleased to see that Ben's attitude to this act of (what?) was simply to ask where they should build another one. His father pondered on the subject of ownership of castles in the sand - the builders own neither the materials used nor the land on which they are built. All they own are the tools and their own labour, and presumably that's worthless, is it? Too big a question for today, he decided, and concentrated on collecting wet sand to decorate Ben's turrets.

The return journey on the train threw up a bizarre sight. Another yacht, nearer this time but still apparently sailing through fields, had

VOTE

BREXIT

PARTY

writ very large indeed on its mainsail. Was it an official party advertisement or had some enterprising (or misguided) yachtie done it for himself? And where had he (surely it had to be a he?) found those monster sized letters to sew/stick on the sail? Puzzled, Ben looked at his father for an explanation.

'Message for grownups,' Paul said. There was no way that he was going to introduce the word politics and, luckily, Ben didn't pursue it further. Odd though that this message-on-a-sail came from a boating person since the restriction free ability to sail to other European countries was, for the more adventurous yachtie, a major benefit of EC membership.

It was just before 5 p.m. when he delivered his happy but tired son to Debbie. 'You've had a nice day I see,' she laughed as Ben ran past her.

'Sandcastles. Fish and Chips. Train,' the boy shouted in reply.

An economical bullet point answer, thought Paul before saying. 'He had a child sized portion of fish and chips for lunch, but it was still quite a plateful, he may not need much in the way of supper.'

'OK. Same again next week?' she asked then added, 'and what if the weather is bad?'

'I've thought of that, we'll go to the Time and Tide Museum at Yarmouth if the weather's not beachworthy.'

She nodded. 'See you next week then.'

'Plan A. Plan A. Plan A,' he muttered, happily, as he cycled back to Sandpiper. 'Paul can do bullet point answers too.' Paul, Ben and Boat take on the world.

Early Friday evening he was grubbing around in Sandpiper's battery compartment when he heard the dyke gate shutting. Looking up he saw Emma and crossed the gangplank to greet her with a smile saying. 'Miss Delicious visits one of her men!'

She half smiled in return. 'There's something I need to talk about, can we go inside?'

He put the kettle on and sat opposite her in the main cabin. She took his hands in hers, looked into his face and before she spoke he knew she was here to say goodbye. The face to face version of Dear John.

'I've had a job offer. An old school friend who's a qualified accountant is a junior partner in a well-established Cambridge practice. As long as I've passed the foundation course, they are willing to take me on as a clerk allowing me Wednesdays off to study for the professional exams. It's the old-fashioned route to qualification. I'll obviously take longer than a full-time student to pass them all but have the advantage that the practical element of training will be complete when I do pass, so it won't take any longer overall to become qualified. And I'm going to take up the offer.'

'You are well rated by all teachers on the course, you'll pass OK. This is a bit of a shock though ... it's too far to commute on a daily basis, isn't it?'

'Long term, yes. I can commute for a week or two, but I think the practice expect me to commit to them by moving in or around Cambridge. And I don't want to spend ten or twelve hours a week in transit.'

'What about your husband whose name I don't even know I realise now?'

'Mark. I've told him. His first response was to think we'd sell up and go our separate ways splitting a small, positive I hope, balance 50-50. Which is fine by me of course.'

'And us, if there is an us?'

'There is and I was obviously hoping we could continue while I studied here but I have to take this opportunity even though the big downside is that I will lose you.' She must have thought that this sounded too harsh a statement, so she tried to lighten it by adding, with an anxious smile, 'both lose you and have to pay Cambridge prices!'

'And suffer Cambridge traffic. Part of my mind is racing along thinking of ways we could still see each other - a place halfway between - visits on alternate weekends - but the other the part of me knows this won't happen. I'm committed to being here for my son and you'll be committed to having to work hard for a professional qualification on a part time basis. And qualifications earned by studying at the kitchen table may be traditional, but they've never been easy. As things stand, the strain of trying to continue as us would almost certainly part us, and the downcurve will be unbearable.'

'I agree, it would be awful but in the happiest of my memories there will always be Paul and Emma.

You were my first lover and you have shown me that I am a person worthy of being loved and cared for by someone like yourself, someone I could talk to and be proud of as well as having sex with. I needed what you have given me and if you've been acting then you deserve an Oscar.'

'You know I have not been acting and you are right. It is good for someone to know they are worthy of love and care from the person they are attracted to and respect. You have been equally good for me; I just wish it had been for longer.'

In silence they stood and hugged tightly. His subconscious must have thought that ending on a light note would bring as little pain as could be hoped for, eventually therefore he found himself saying. 'Well, at least you've rectified the two faults, not omissions, you mentioned when we first met in the Costa.'

She drew back a little to look at him, tearful but smiling as she remembered her words. 'Rectified plus covers it.'

'Emma and Paul enjoyed a two night stand,' he intoned, as if reading a radio announcement. At the same time his thumb gently brushed a tear from her cheek.

'But it's been much more than a two night stand, hasn't it?'

'Much more, and I am so grateful to you for

making it happen,' he replied.

She was still for a few moments then hugged him hard before drawing back and kissing his lips. 'It's time to go, my lover. Please don't walk me to the car. Stand in the cockpit so I can look back from the gate and see you on Sandpiper.'

At the dyke gate she turned and looked at them for a moment then was gone. At that point, with the need for lightness of touch now over, the absolute finality of her departure bore down on him, bringing with it an acute sense of loss. He would never be with another woman so inhibited - they could talk about anything, and nothing seemed to be out of bounds in their lovemaking. He supposed that in the long run familiarity would have dulled their pleasure. Well, he'd never know now, perhaps it was as well to have nothing but these few high peaks to remember. He further supposed that their parting removed one of the complications from his current life, but it was his sense of loss that coloured the rest of the evening.

SIX
2039:
Preveza to Ormos Kopraina

Preveza is a town on the northeast coast of mainland Greece. It is a busy town on Saturday mornings, but he has their week's shopping in three bags and is walking back to the boat by midday. April to October is the season for those (mostly Northern Europeans) who keep their boat in the Greek Ionian. Arriving at the local airport white legged and wintery they leave looking like circumnavigators. They are a necessary part of the local economy.

It is June so the inner harbour is crowded, and their elderly yacht is banked alongside a larger boat on pier 3. Victoria waits for him in her usual spot in the cockpit, watching as he takes off his sandals before barefooting to and fro across the neighbouring boat's foredeck until all the shopping is aboard their own boat. He's learned the hard way that in this situation you move your footwear across first - years ago now one of the harbour dogs had run off with his left sandal as it sat invitingly on the quay. He'd found its chewed remains a week later.

For a sailor one of the many attractions of the Greek Ionian is the predictability of its thermal winds. A westerly usually starts around 1:30 p.m., building up to a 20/25 knot strength until dying down around 8 p.m. Here in the Gulf of Amvrakakia there's often a very light north-easterly from just after dawn to around 11 a.m. He's taken to using the strong afternoon wind to sail in one passage the 20 miles to the far end of the gulf, anchoring at the north end in Ormos Kopraina. They would typically stay there for a couple of nights then use the light early morning wind to sail day by day, anchorage by anchorage, slowly back to Preveza. Occasionally they varied this itinerary and either sailed south to Levkas, Itheka and beyond or north to Paxos, Corfu and the Greek mainland near the Albanian border.

Now and again a dominant weather system takes over for a few days, typically bringing much rain and strong south-easterly winds. They usually sought a sheltered anchorage at the first sign of the south-easterly and he would rig up the rainwater collecting system as soon as they were anchored. Rain tastes better than tap water these days and, if there were no near neighbours, he could also strip off for a shower from the sky.

He stows the food and drink and eats a quick

lunch by which time the afternoon wind has set in. He switches on the electric engine's isolator and revises the mooring warps so that they are easy to cast off. With just a faint whine from the electric outboard motor they move slowly astern, past the pier end then turn and head forward towards the town quay. He is well practised at this and has both sails raised and pulling and the engine off within two minutes. They turn east to sail down the gulf.

For a boat on passage the west end of the gulf is comparatively narrow with the airport on flat land to the south. Low hills with a few small settlements are to the north. Here, shoreline features include what would be a beautiful bay except for the rusting hulk of an abandoned coaster. That and what look like garden sheds on pontoons powered by outboard engines, the sure sign of a fish farm. A spoiled bay, an eyesore to most northern Europeans he supposes but this is Greece, a country that's been good to him. A country with its relatively small population spread over many islands and an extensive mainland. Centralisation is not as marked here meaning that towns like Preveza can still supply or make pretty much anything.

Greece had not been so hard hit as the hitherto more developed northern European countries when the trend for independence accelerated in the late 2020s. Belgium had split into French speaking

Wallonia and Flemish speaking Flanders. Wales and Scotland became independent nations. With much bitterness Ireland eventually united last year, 2038. England broke into a loose association of self-governing regions such as Cornwall, East Anglia and Estuaria. In mainland Europe, Catalonia and Brittany became independent. The Netherlands developed similarly to the now not United Kingdom with Holland, Friesland, Brabant and Zeeland now featuring on maps which were being redrawn annually. The widespread Greek towns and islands had always had a degree of autonomy and were used to coping locally without great need to court central government investment. The result being that this former beggar of Europe had become a role model of how to do things on a low-tech and local basis. In a high-down listing of metres of shoreline per head of population Greece must be close to the top. It's a country with a great deal of margin, thus the perfect place for those whose natural instincts are to live on the edges of a country. He's put a lot of effort into learning the language and can now shop as economically as a local. He'll always be an outsider of course but has been here long enough for many locals to treat him as one of their own. This is a level of belonging he can cope with. A marginal man but an accepted one.

A medium haul passenger aircraft with landing gear down crosses ahead of them. It is Saturday so the plane is inbound from countries which used to form the UK. Preveza airport is organised to take flights to and from what was the UK on Tuesdays and Saturdays. Mondays and Fridays are down to what was Germany and the Netherlands, Wednesdays and Sundays to and from Scandanavia, Thursdays to and from what was once France and Belgium. He presumes this organisation is to do with which foreign languages are spoken by airport staff. And perhaps also to do with ensuring that the staff are part-timers without holiday entitlement, etc. Today's employment method.

A short dogleg then the gulf opens out to perhaps three or four miles wide and the terrain does an about face. To the north now it is flat and in the distance they can see a village with a small harbour. Use fingers to frame this view and you could be sailing on the Ijsselmeer in what was once the Netherlands. To the south it is much more like the traditional Greece, olive groves on hills framing the three wide bays which form their stopping points on the slow journey back to Preveza over the next few days.

The afternoon wind is up to its full strength now and they make six knots plus, rolling in the following waves. He reefs the foresail down to about half size and sheets it hard in, helping to balance the full mainsail on this broad reach. Victoria does not like the resulting rolling, yawing motion and retires to the cabin, lying as low as possible, close to the boat's roll centre.

On they sail as the gulf gradually narrows from the north. Water depth decreases as they approach the eastern end of the gulf. A pod of dolphin regularly hunt in this area. His boys he calls them, convinced that they use passing yachts as part of their fish herding technique. He hears them exhaling and a second later seven or eight are alongside. Their athleticism and their silvery wake as they break surface always fills him with joy. He shouts words of greeting, gestures with his free arm and marvels yet again at how such small body movements produce such apparently effortless speeds. He wonders what these intelligent creatures think of him. Is he seen as part of the boat (or the boat part of him) or as a creature on a boat? He has no way of knowing but all his senses tell him that they are enjoying this interaction. Victoria watches through the cabin window, they frighten her, but she has to look.

The dolphin leave as suddenly as they came. The eastern end of the gulf is here now, and they turn north on a close reach for the final mile and a half into Ormos Kopraina, anchoring in smooth, shallow water between the two tiny harbours at the northernmost point. They are regulars here and within a few minutes he hears the increasingly rare sound of a diesel engine. Looking to the south he sees a small boat approaching. Only commercial shipping and fishing vessels are allowed to use diesel engines these days. The small boat grows larger and he recognises her as that of Christos. Fishermen such as Christos are still allowed to use diesel engines as long as fishing is their main source of income. Leisure fishermen, and there are many of them locally, have to use electric engines, oars or sails. Mostly it's the first two so they don't tend to stray as far from base as they used to. One or two of the more forward-thinking owners of traditional caiques have fitted lugsails on short masts but most leisure fishermen just use oars when the wind is with them and motor when it is not.

He and Christos shout greetings to each other as the fishing boat passes on her way into harbour. He and Victoria are known and accepted here.

SEVEN

2019

Like most college teachers in the final two or three weeks of the summer term, Paul's classroom hours went down and admin hours went up. Students of the accountant's foundation course sat their six exams. Three days' worth of a three-hour paper in the morning followed by a three-hour paper in the afternoon. After which, presumably punch drunk, they went back to where they came from leaving their teachers to mark their papers, justify their marks to external examiners and finally sit in a meeting where each student was graded. Emma and Adebola had both done well, as had his icemaiden, Briony Barton-Jones. Everyone in the meeting smiled as G T Tyson BCom MA FCA ETC said her name and Paul wondered if being so gloriously attractive would be a help or a hindrance to her professional life. It shouldn't matter of course but ... whatever, he wished her well. The two students he thought may fail his exam did so. Luckily for him they'd also failed some of their other five papers and the meeting agreed that the course leader should counsel them onto a lower level course rather than encourage resits, an unenviable task and certainly one well beyond Paul's own interpersonal skills. He was leaving at the end of the meeting when Tyson called him back, telling him that his performance review was on Friday at 0900 in the principal lecturer's office.

On Sandpiper that evening he thought through how he was going to deal with the performance review. If he and Ben were heading off over the horizon then the review didn't matter at all, why even attend? But he had to attend, it was necessary to keep up the appearance of wanting to retain his job and if something went wrong with Plan A ... Yes, he'd have to eat the undoubtedly large helping of humble pie required by a contrite teacher.

Friday 0900. Paul sat on one side of a table with Tyson, Geoff Nutt (the course leader) and John Barnes, principal lecturer in math on the other. Tyson described the deputation he'd received at the end of Paul's disintegrating class and the action he himself had taken by organising the copying of old exam papers followed by telling Paul exactly what was required of him for the final three weeks of the course.

'Is that a fair summary?' Tyson asked, looking at Paul.

It was and it made him seem the idiot of the year. 'Yes, it is, and I'd like to say that I now realise how stupid it was of me to attempt to generate interest by taking such a broad-brush approach that close to their exams. In future I promise that my first focus will be on preparing them for their exams. In fact, I found very satisfying the last three weeks of going through the old papers with the class, as directed by Mr Tyson, and the subsequent atmosphere in the class was excellent, I feel.'

'I agree with that. I took some soundings in the last two weeks and they were very positive,' said Geoff Nutt.

Tyson nodded and turned to Barnes, 'Anything to add, John?'

'Perhaps this is a good moment to remind Paul that the accounting class is at post A level. Some of his colleagues would regard teaching at this level as an upgrade on their current work,' said Barnes, the threat only too clear.

'The point is taken. You can be sure that the focus will be on my performance in the future,' replied Paul. And that's an entire humble pie eaten and a Tyson rear end well licked. What a thought.

Tyson looked at Nutt and Barnes in turn, both of whom nodded. 'Very well Paul. You can continue on the course for the next academic year, but you are on probation. We shall have this meeting again in a year's time. On a personal level, thank you for knuckling down and doing excellent work at the end, the external examiner was well satisfied with the standard of answers on your paper. And I wish you a good summer break, come back refreshed,' Tyson said, breaking into a smile before dismissing him.

Also, over these last weeks of term, Paul and Anneke enjoyed finding out more about each other's background. She'd studied computing at university in Amsterdam and had a long-term relationship with a fellow student which had finally broken down last year. She'd escaped to a job here at college and, at 31, started life again, living in single room campus accommodation during term time then flying back to Holland to stay with her parents in Hoorn during college holidays. She was paid only for term time which seemed grossly unfair to Paul. The term ended and the following day they caught the airport bus, taking longer to travel the four miles of traffic-ridden city streets than the 35 minutes it would take to fly to Amsterdam Schiphol. At Departures they said a lingering goodbye, promising to meet in Hoorn in ten days or so.

From being the centre of attention at set times during each weekday many teachers find the sudden freedom of the first few days of the summer holidays difficult to adjust to. Not so Paul Williams, his first week already mapped out. Boat preparation for the first three days, then access day on Thursday, then move Sandpiper downriver on Friday ready for the 10 a.m. bridge lifts at Great Yarmouth on Saturday. He didn't plan to stop in Yarmouth just continue straight on from the open bridge to the open sea where they would head east for Holland. By Wednesday afternoon Sandpiper was as ready as she would ever be, so he texted his planned departure date and time to the number given by Gunton, receiving a curt reply. 'Make contact when there.'

Access day weather was overcast with light rain predicted in late morning. He and Ben caught the train to Yarmouth spending the morning in the Time and Tide Museum. He had worried that Ben might be quickly bored but the boy was enthusiastic about many of the exhibits, particularly the Breeches Buoy. They lunched at the museum then Ben took him back to the Breeches exhibit. Paul realised that up to this point his son had associated being shot at with being hurt by the shot (what were they letting him watch?) but had now found something that was shot in someone's direction, and done so in an attempt to save their life. Quite a linkage for a four-year-old. From the Time and Tide museum to Haven Bridge where the tide was flooding, and they had time before the train to watch water flow past the thick columns supporting the bridge's opening section. An empty cigarette packet was floating towards the centre of the column and they watched as it neared the column before moving sideways in a graceful arc, literally following the streamlines, and accelerating out of sight below the bridge.

'Faster,' said Ben.

That's my boy he thought but said, 'Yes, the packet and the water it's floating on have to go faster because the column is making the channel more narrow here.' Paul used his hands to demonstrate. 'The columns don't squash the water, but they don't need to, you remember that bonds between water molecules break and reform easily. The water's way of dealing with the obstruction of the column is to go faster around it then slow down again to reform on the other side of the column.' Not one of life's great explanations, he knew, but Ben was smiling.

'Yes,' his son said. A good answer as lately Paul had realised that in this sort of situation Ben's 'yes' means 'yes, I will think about it.'

On the train back to the village Paul explained that he would be away having a nice sail to Holland for two or three weeks. Just as soon as he got back, he'd phone Mummy and make arrangements to see Ben as soon as possible. His son looked hurt for a moment so he added, 'and think how lovely it will be to see each other again.'

'Yes Daddy,' Ben said and reached for his father's hand, the mini engineer becoming a small boy looking for reassurance, which he got in spades. The train rumbled on and this week they saw no political message-on-a-sail. At Ben's home he kissed the top of his son's head and reminded Debbie about the cruise to Holland, saying he'd return in three weeks or less. She had not forgotten and wished him good sailing before closing the door. Outside the house the classic MGB gleamed as before.

On Friday morning he tied the gangplank to his mooring posts hammered into the dyke's bank, scrambled back on board, freed the remaining ropes and used the engine in astern to exit the dyke. They were en route.

In the light westerly/south-westerly they could sail only slowly but it helped that the tide had just started ebbing. They progressed to the chain tracked Reedham Ferry which was busy, a queue having formed on both sides of the river. He was cautious as usual, motor sailing quickly past when the ferry was taking its next load. Engine on again at Reedham where, sails down, they stemmed the tide for ten minutes until the Lowestoft train crossed and the bridge was able to swing open shortly after. The wind, southwesterly now, continued and they sailed on for another six miles or so before mooring at the Berney Arms quay. Just three and a half miles from the first of the Yarmouth bridges, it was a favourite Friday night mooring for those going to sea the following day. Two other sea-going yachts were already there and they were soon joined by two of the Mermaid Cove Marina's finest, gleaming gin palaces of 39- and 45-feet length according to the lettering on their superstructure. A superstructure sprouting radar scanners, satellite domes and aerials of all types. Paul tried to think of alternative words to conspicuous consumption and failed. Those well-worn words fitted perfectly.

Around 7 p.m. the sea-goers wandered down to the Berney Arms pub in case it had opened since their last visit. It hadn't but they rapidly got around to the inevitable 'where are you off to' conversation. This time tomorrow crew on the other two yachts were aiming to be eating a fish and chip supper in the Harbour Inn at Southwold. Travelling at over twenty knots the crew of the larger gin palace expected to be dining in central Amsterdam tomorrow evening. When they were dining Sandpiper would be about a third of the way to Holland, at best. Crew on the other gin palace had not been to sea in their boat before and were apprehensive about the six-mile passage to Lowestoft.

Saturday morning and Sandpiper was away early sailing over Breydon Water, slowly at first against the last of the flood tide then more quickly as the ebb took over. The two other yachts did the same and they arrived close to the Breydon Bridge within a few minutes of each other, lowering sails and tying to posts to stream with the ebb until called to be ready for the opening. A few minutes before 10 a.m. two large bow waves changed very quickly from seeming far away to slowing down nearby. The gin palaces had arrived.

Both bridges opened without problems and Paul motored at not much more than tickover as the now well-established ebb swept them towards the sea. South of the harbour entrance he raised full sail, cut the engine and turned east to start the passage to Ijmuiden, the seaport of Amsterdam, some 104 miles away. From there one lock and 13 miles of canal should see them in central Amsterdam. The wind was around twelve knots in strength and the seas showed just an occasional white horse. As benign a start as he could wish for.

As usual it took him some hours to find his sea legs though Sandpiper was in her stride straight away, loping along at three and a half to four knots for the rest of the day until the evening when the wind eased and finally died when they were around a third of the way to Ijmuiden. He left the sails up, in the hope that the wind would return soon. It also made them more visible to other vessels, so they were less likely to be mown down by a ship with an inattentive crew.

It was truly dark at midnight and there were no

clouds. No light pollution either so he lay out on the cockpit seating and gazed upward at a spectacle Sky at Night viewers would envy. In the past he'd shown no interest in stars and planets so was unable to differentiate a great bear from a not so great one. He did know though that anyone wishing to feel insignificant could do worse than isolate themselves in the middle of the North Sea on a night such as this.

Although a wind may disappear altogether, its effect on the sea does not and Sandpiper rolled uncomfortably in the swell, sails slatting uselessly from side to side. They didn't have enough petrol to continue the passage under engine, but Paul decided to start the engine and motor east for two hours to see if they could get out of this hole in the wind. Foolishly he added a little more time, and a little more and the engine had been on for three and a half hours by the time he switched it off. They were now fifteen miles closer to Ijmuiden and five and a half litres of petrol lighter, and still windless. At best they now had petrol for just four hours of motoring. To be safe they would have to use sailpower alone to get within twelve miles of Ijmuiden. He cursed himself for being an idiot and the weather gods for being worse.

They were stuck there, windless, for thirty hours. Stuck there meaning in the same bit of water. Relative to the seabed below the bit of water on which

Sandpiper floated moved southish for sixish hours then northish for sixish hours then ... the relentless tidal cycle continued. At the north end of the cycle he could just make out a wellhead or similar oil industry structure and once, waking from a doze, he saw that they were frighteningly close to the eastern edge of a North Sea fishing fleet, eighteen trawlers a couple of miles away and coming slowly towards them. Worried and tired, his imagination could not rid itself of the image of the whole fleet pulling one gigantic net and Sandpiper joining a few thousand fish in it. So, another litre of petrol was used before he convinced himself that the fleet would miss them.

He knew about tidal sailing in theory but never had the opportunity to try it until now. The theory has it that in this situation Sandpiper's movement north or south with the tidal stream results in a very small airflow at about ninety degrees to the sail - assuming her bow was pointing roughly east. Combine this with heeling the boat, and thus the sails, to leeward and it should be possible to generate some tiny forward movement. He tried it for the three hours of maximum tidal flow, but Sandpiper proved too heavy to take advantage, unsurprising really given that the water movement relative to the seabed was around 1.3 knots at best. However, he saw enough to convince himself that the method would work with a lightweight and sweetly shaped boat, the opposite of Sandpiper.

Eventually there came a tiny breath from the south. Inside the cabin he moved a few heavy items to the port side and in the cockpit he leaned to that same side holding out the boom with one hand while the other stretched to get his fingertips on the tiller. This induced heeling helped them to make progress, slow at first but building and he was soon able to adopt a more comfortable position as over a couple of hours their speed rose to just over four knots. In the afternoon their progress started to slow as the wind died down again. In the evening it left them wallowing once more but was that smudge on the eastern horizon actually Ijmuiden? On the phone his navigation app said just under 10 miles to the harbour entrance, just about reachable under engine if he was particularly gentle with the throttle. Darkness fell as they motored east. Approaching a harbour you don't know after dark is not one of life's calming moments. In Europe harbour entrances have a green light to starboard and a red to port. It should be easy to see the lights and pass between them. And it is easy for those able to ignore the entire towns' worth of other lights filling their sight, including the same red and green of the towns many traffic lights. To make it worse for Paul he saw a cruise ship anchored a couple of miles offshore, presumably waiting for the harbour's largest lock to be prepared for entry. It was a terrible cliché to say that something's lit up like a

Christmas tree but he didn't care, that's exactly what the cruise ship looked like. And it seemed to be between them and the entrance.

Suddenly he pulled the tiller hard over to miss the inshore fishing boat he hadn't seen until almost too late. Becoming confused now, he went back to heading slowly east, passing just south of the cruise ship. The scene seemed to be changing, there was a harbour wall ahead and its lower surface had saw teeth. No, that's stupid, surely that's a wave pattern? He concentrated. They were saw teeth! He turned ninety degrees south and faced the same wall. In a panic he turned a further ninety degrees to be moving west, away from shore, but the wall and its teeth was still in front of them. He shifted the gear lever to neutral and closed his eyes for a minute. Opening them he found the scene back to where it was five minutes ago. He found the phone and swiped the screen. They were two miles south of the entrance. Would they have enough fuel? With bits of this and that he wedged up one end of the fuel tank such that its supply tube could get at every scrap of petrol. They motored north for the entrance. Hope surged inside him as he realised that the tidal flow was in their favour, a hope soon dashed as he saw to his horror that the cruise ship had turned and was also heading for the harbour entrance but very, very slowly. She had right of way of course so he turned the engine off and drifted north in the helpful tide, watching as the large ship manoeuvred herself into a position such that she could aim straight for the lock. When Sandpiper was clear to go into harbour he started the engine and headed in. The engine stuttered twice but recovered in lumpy waves just outside the entrance. The sea was calmer inside and he throttled back to just over tickover, willing the fuel to last just ten more minutes. They took the buoyed channel into the Seaport Marina and, a couple of minutes later, occupied the only vacant spot left on the fuel berth. It was just after 1 a.m. when he sat in the cockpit, sweating with relief and downing a mug of coffee of heart-stopping strength.

'Dag meneer,' Paul awoke with a start to see a grinning man in a marina tee shirt leaning into the cockpit. They were alone on the fuel berth. 'I fuelled the others first to let you sleep,' the man said.

'Dank je wel mineer,' Paul replied then, as he couldn't remember the Dutch for thirty, he asked for that many litres in English. He paid and they wished each other Tot Ziens. Half an hour later Sandpiper and another three boats entered the Kleinensluis and locked through to the Noord Zee Canaal. Hoping for a berth in Sixhaven, a choice yacht harbour on the edge of central Amsterdam he decided not to sail but to motor so that they could time their arrival to be around 1 p.m. when there was a good chance of getting a berth. He knew competition for berths there became hot later in the day. So it proved and they were allocated a good one at the east end of the yacht basin. From here it was just a three-minute walk to the free ferry across the water to the central railway station and from there another ten minutes to some beautiful parts of old Amsterdam.

Before that though he had a beer in the yacht club bar where he got directions to the nearest supermarket. By early evening Sandpiper was stocked with fresh fruit and veg plus two boxes of red wine, the first of which tasted like fruit juice, but he didn't care. A happy man cooked his evening meal watching late arriving boats cramming themselves into any space that looked remotely like being big enough to house them. Well before dusk you could walk straight across any part of the yacht harbour treading only on boats. At dusk he called Anneke's number, looking forward to her excitement at finding he was here. The number rang but was unanswered.

Sandpiper safely secured, he slept long and decided in the morning to allow himself two days of tourism here. It was still good weather and in the afternoon he walked in the sun along narrow, cobbled streets running beside canals. Above him old townhouses stood tall, their merchant past denoted by cranes jutting out immediately below the eaves. Oh, he could live here. He could live here, he knew. He wondered if a job was possible. It would have to pay well to be able to afford to live in a capital city and also cover the weekly air fare back to the UK for his time with Ben. All very unlikely of course but there was an atmosphere in Amsterdam that appealed to him. Yes, he'd love to live here.

Visiting Amsterdam's red-light district was pretty much obligatory, so much so that many tourist brochures gave directions. In the evening he went there and found that living flesh advertised in front windows was more than a bit of a turn off. He felt sorry for the sex workers parading their wares, resignedly adopting 'sexy' poses (which he found anything but) while constantly keeping an eye out for punters heading for their door. A dispiriting visit to a place only around a hundred metres from where he'd been happy that afternoon, but a million miles away in every other respect.

He tried Anneke's phone again the following day but there was still no answer. Away from home but forgot to take the phone? Or did he have the wrong number? An internet search revealed that a few Anneke Wilders had a presence on the web but none of them his Anneke. He thought he might have to ask around in Hoorn and how pathetic that sounded but he couldn't think of anything better at that moment.

In the afternoon he treated himself to more canal walks, again enjoying that feeling of affinity with the city. In early evening he topped up the fresh food stocks and just before dusk took a check on the mooring situation. They were blocked in by just one French flagged yacht of roughly the same size as Sandpiper whose skipper would be only too pleased to move to let them out at 8 a.m. tomorrow, then get into Sandpiper's much better berth before anyone else could.

At 9 a.m. the following day they approached the Oranjesluis, the lock allowing access to the open waters of the Markermeer. It was coming up time to make contact with Gunton and Jan's associates so he decided to sail straight for Enkhuizen, after which it would be just a short passage west to Hoorn and (he hoped) Anneke. After the North Sea the shallow waters of the Markermeer provided a short choppy motion in the southwesterly wind though Sandpiper was happy enough in it, sailing wing and wing for four hours to reach Enkhuizen's outer harbour in early afternoon. There was plenty of activity around the lock and they had to wait half an hour before a place could be found in it. Then they were through, having access now to the town's harbours and the Ijsselmeer stretching out in front of them. At the far end of town, they turned to the north and entered the

Compieshaven and made for the Zuider Zee Museum, anchoring just off its quay. The museum itself was a re-creation of an old East India Company harbour and village in the northeast corner of the Compieshaven. He had feared it would be crowded but only five other boats were at anchor nearby.

In the small hours he was woken by a knocking on Sandpiper's hull followed by the unmistakeable thump then the roll of the boat telling him a large person was coming aboard. As Paul scrambled dozily out of his berth the cabin door opened and the resulting space became occupied by what looked like a very large man who said, 'Paul Williams?' Struggling into his trousers, about as ready as a dead elephant to defend his boat, Paul grunted his assent.

'It's after 0200 so it's now Tuesday. Later today take a mooring at the haven,' his thumb pointed to the marina behind him, 'for two nights and the following day, that's Wednesday, walk into town at 1000 hours for sightseeing, shopping or whatever and don't return until 1400 hours at the earliest. Understood?' The man might be superthug size, but he spoke excellent English.

'Yes, understood,' Paul replied weakly.

The man turned and, despite his size, deftly stepped back into his dinghy and expertly rowed towards the public slipway. So, this was to be the placing of the consignment Paul thought then realised that the man hadn't told him to leave the cabin door unlocked. Clearly, he'd have to leave it that way if they were to stow the consignment inside.

On Wednesday he did as instructed and walked into Enkhuizen at 10 a.m. Both as a sailor and as a man, the Anglo-Irish author Erskine Childers was one of Paul's heroes so he walked to the far end of the Westerstraat where he knew some of the street scenes from the film The Riddle of the Sands had been shot, finding the church Klara and her mother had attended and that odd, spiked globe thing overhanging the street, waiting to impale some passing innocent, a category in which Paul no longer qualified. Later, returning to the boat with shopping, he found no obvious signs of entry or stowage and assumed that something or someone had prevented it.

He decided to stay on to see if it would happen on the following day but at 2 a.m. there was another visit from the big man, this time on foot. telling him he needed to be back on the Broads in ten days' time.

So, the consignment was stowed then, 'Where is the stuff hidden?' Paul asked but the man shook his head and left.

Later that day, after breakfast, he used the phone's Windfinder forecasting app to discover that a northeasterly airstream was predicted to cover the

North Sea from here to East Anglia in eight days' time. Any forecast that far ahead was tentative to say the least, but he'd have to plan for it. Sandpiper needed to be within striking distance of Ijmuiden to take advantage of this wind but that still left five or six days for tourism. Early on Thursday morning he set sail for Hoorn, the other old East India Company town recommended by Jan. It was also where Anneke's parents lived and he hoped she might be there this time. He would call her number as soon as he'd showered and made himself what passed for presentable.

With Sandpiper safely at anchor once more he rowed into Hoorn and almost immediately found the bronze statues of children playing on the sea wall, the Sea Mice of Hoorn. They formed a moving tribute to the fate of children kidnapped to work on boats fishing or transporting goods on the North and South Seas - the Zuider Zee being the name for the sea south of the Friesian Islands to the north, Den Helder to the west and Harlingen to the east. Now enclosed and tamed by massive sea walls and renamed the Ijsselmeer.

It was not lost on Paul that Ben was about to join the sea mice. Did they ever get home or did they have to work the boats for the rest of their (possibly short) lives? And suffer abuse, or is that just a modern preoccupation he asked himself?

He was contemplating this when there was a sudden shout, 'Paul!'

He half turned to find Anneke three or four metres away, light coloured shorts and tee shirt emphasising her tanned body. With a shopping bag in each hand, she looked delighted to see him. And that was mutual, he strode forward and hugged her as if they'd loved each other for years. He eventually let go and they kissed. 'You look delicious, absolutely edible!' he said, 'and it's amazing that we just happen to meet here at this spot, at this time, on this day, as if pre-ordained. And I was going to call you as soon as I'd used the marina showers.'

'A shower quite soon would be a good idea,' she paused then continued, 'certainly before tonight. I will tell my mother that we have a guest for dinner. Someone who needs to be well fed or he will eat her only daughter. Now I must get back with this food before it melts but meet me here, looking like a hunk of the year contestant, at 6 p.m. And be warned, my father will almost certainly mention Brexit.'

Showered, shaved and wearing the most respectable clothes he could muster he stood beside the sea mice, deliberately early in order to be with the kidnapped children. Could he really do this to Ben? The effect on Debbie would be devastating. Presumably parents of the sea mice would have known that children playing in the harbour area were in danger of being stolen. Perhaps life was not so precious then? Was this sort of outcome just accepted as a risk? In those days a number of children would not have survived to an age where they would be seen as being of use on a working vessel. Suddenly he was hugged from behind.

'I was looking for a hunk of the year contestant, but you will have to do! It is time for trial by parent. Despite everything I told them they are looking forward to meeting you. Come,' she said, taking his arm.

'What exactly have you told them about me?'

'The truth. That you are four years older than me, divorced with a four-year-old son, living on your boat which you have sailed here to see me. Teacher at the college, an eligible man lusted over by most of the female staff in the computer department. A man I quite like.' She squeezed his arm and smiled at him as she said those last few words.

'The quite liking is mutual. And I must remember to flex my muscles and leer at your female colleagues when next in the computer department.' He'd kept the tone as light as hers but was no further forward. He would have to play this evening by ear, which he knew was not one of his talents. Anneke's parents may just view him as one of her friends from college or they may view him as a potential son-in-law, someone to be assessed. Christ, if only they knew what he was. If only *he* knew what he was.

Her parents lived in a modest-sized townhouse not far from the centre of Hoorn. She ushered him through the door first. At the other end of the hall a woman turned and he could not hide his shock as he looked at another Anneke. An older one. An older but still beautiful Anneke.

The woman laughed. 'You are surprised to see an old Anneke,' she said in excellent English.

'No, it is delight at meeting an older but still beautiful Anneke,' he said, smiling broadly as he moved forward and offered his hand.

She took his hand and at the same time pulled him forward for a kiss on both cheeks. 'So,' she said, stepping back and nodding, 'you are Paul. I hope you like seafood, Paul.'

He was starting to assure her he did when a door opened to his side and Anneke's father stepped out to greet him with a handshake. About the same height as himself but bulkier with thinning fair hair. And a deep voice, 'Anneke told me you were sure to be wearing a Manchester United shirt so I have my Ajax one here to change into if necessary.'

Paul had never even been to Manchester but knew United had supporters all over the world. 'Your lovely daughter has a terrible sense of humour, sir. I don't support any particular football team,' he replied, 'but of course we all know of Ajax and the total football associated with Johan Cryff.'

'In that case you have made a very good start with us, Paul. Now I shall introduce you to a small glass of Genever before we sit down to eat.'

Anneke butted in. 'Just before you do that, I would like to mention that my parent's names are Hans and Henriette. They were obviously so stunned by your appearance that they forgot what they are called.'

The cordial and relaxed start set the tone for the evening and he quickly felt at ease with this lively and confident Dutch family. During the meal Paul learned that Anneke's father ran a wholesale business dealing in flowers, mostly for export. It wasn't until they were taking coffee that Hans asked why the British disliked fellow Europeans so much that they voted Brexit.

Paul replied, 'I don't think the vote was intended to be anti-European. I think it was more a case of people wanting their country back. You could think of it as a cry from the heart. A desire to walk down the street and see others who look similar to you and who speak the same language. A desire to say that and not be branded a racist. A wanting to have British football teams owned by British people and buildings on British soil owned by British people. Wanting to avoid seeing mosques everywhere. Wanting to stop the National Health Service becoming privatised. And a desire for what might be seen as greater security brought about by less variety. It's all far too late of course, none of these desires can be met but the referendum provided an opportunity to rebel against something most of the establishment were happy with. And a small majority of the public took that opportunity to hit back. Whether or not it was sensible is another matter, I've heard it likened to losing your keys in a dark street then looking for them in the next one where it is well lit.'

He looked around the table. 'Sorry, that was a rambling answer. I was trying to say that the vote was not against fellow Europeans per se.'

'An interesting answer though. Your colonial history bites back, as does ours,' said Henriette.

'I see what you mean but leaving will hit your economy hard,' added Hans.

Paul smiled at his hosts, 'Yes.'

At 10.30 p.m. he decided that the evening had gone well enough and that he'd leave while apparently ahead. He thanked Hans and Henriette for a most enjoyable evening, telling them that he now knew who Anneke had inherited her beauty and her admirable character from and that he was so pleased to have met them.

At the door Anneke hugged him. 'That went well, you flatterer.'

'Thank heavens for that, I was terrified of making a bad impression.'

'No, the opposite, I think. I was proud of you. Can we go on our mini cruise starting tomorrow?' she asked.

'Yes please. I'll bring Sandpiper to the yacht club quay for whatever time you say.'

They agreed to meet by the sea mice at 10 a.m. then they kissed, broke away looking at each other then kissed again, more urgently.

In a turmoil he walked back to Sandpiper's dinghy. What had he been doing this evening? He and Anneke were heading for a destination wholly incompatible with Plan A, which was still the most important factor in his life, wasn't it? If it was then he could not fall completely for Anneke and yet seemed to be doing so. And here he was, this other person, the criminal Paul Edward Williams, a man whose boat carried a consignment of illicit drugs, diamonds or something prison worthy. At the moment he was playing at least three roles, far too many for someone of his character, or anyone perhaps but how would he know what others could cope with? If Plan A was foremost then Anneke was an unnecessary complication. He should just set sail for Norfolk first thing in the morning, leaving a text on Anneke's mobile to stop her packing a bag for their mini cruise which would not happen. Christ, if only he hadn't agreed to do the bloody 'run' for Gunton and Jan he might be able to find a way of having both Anneke and Ben in his life, he was sure they would get on. He was confident that she would be a kind and loving occasional stepmother to the boy. Rowing back to Sandpiper he knew he could not let her down, they would have their two days of sailing and he would make sure she enjoyed them. He couldn't see how at the moment but there may be a way through the mess he'd got himself into.

EIGHT

2039:

Ormos Kopraina to Palioumilou

It is the evening of their second day there. The sun is below the horizon now, but they continue to sit in the warm cockpit. The afternoon wind has gone too, it will be another quiet night here at anchor in Ormos Kopraina. Two miles away to the east lights in the village of Menhidion are becoming defined, as are those of Arta further away up the hill to the north.

He's discovered a late flowering talent for practical electronics and it pleases him that his self-made anchor light (cobbled together entirely from bits thrown away by others) switches itself on at dusk and off once more at dawn while using a minimum amount of battery power. Sadly for his finances there's no great call for this skill in the Preveza area of northwest Greece. Or anywhere else these days he suspects.

In fact, it's nearly two years since he last earned anything. For some time before that he was able to get occasional employment with Eirini, the young

Greek lady running Ionian Breeze, a local company chartering yachts from Preveza's inner harbour. He didn't want to leave Victoria overnight but was able to skipper a one-day yacht charter, a fun day sail that nobody seems to want any more. Eirini's business soon grew to be Europe wide and she moved her base to Germany. He admired her and was delighted at her success. She was persistent, determined and had all the people skills he did not.

These days he and Victoria spend the winter aboard, mostly with the boat tied up alongside in the inner harbour in Preveza. This used to provide the opportunity to charge a small monthly fee for keeping an eye on other boats left in the water nearby, their owners having flown home for the winter. 'Keeping an eye on' is called guardinage (Gar Din Ahge) locally but, whatever it's called, global warming has put paid to it as a means of income - boats' bottoms resemble a coral reef after just one month static in the inner harbour, let alone the whole winter. Those who used to leave their boats in the water are now much more inclined to have them expensively lifted out and stored at one of the three dry ports bunched together just south of the town, conveniently near the airport. When the water warms up in late spring, he does their own boats' bottom, a grim couple of days work with mask, snorkel and scraper. The result being less fouling for the boat's bottom and more for his due to the inevitable bout of Montezuma's Revenge.

At first light the following day he raises the mainsail and then the anchor. He lets the boat drift astern then bears away towards the east while unrolling the foresail. They turn and broad reach slowly south in the light morning wind from the northeast. It's six miles or so to Palioumilou, their first anchorage on the return journey to Preveza. They are making just one and a half knots but he perseveres, setting the autopilot while he makes breakfast which they eat in the cockpit. The wind dies and they have to use the electric engine for the last two miles.

Summer months in hot countries carry the threat of forest fires. Northwest Greece has two ancient twin piston engined seaplanes which form part of their fire fighting force. He tends to see them only two or three times a year but it's in this part of the gulf the old yellow seaplanes roar down as if to land but instead scoop up water into their bellies before flying off to dump their load onto a fire. These planes are quite small, and it seems at first glance to be a gloriously inefficient method of firefighting but, short of a fool proof way of invoking rain, how else can you dump water exactly where it is needed on a large forest fire? As long as they have fuel the two planes keep returning to scoop up more and he's often thought about what, if any, collision regulations apply to 'meetings' with vessels in the vicinity. Presumably the pilot's survival instinct shows him/her where it is safe to pick up water. Certainly this is not a busy part of the gulf so perhaps worry is necessary.

Past the large fish farm at the western end of the bay he drops anchor off the deserted end of the beach where there is good shelter from waves generated by the afternoon wind, which will set in soon. At this time of the year the Ionian sun is strong and solar panels on their coach roof will soon put back into the batteries the power used to finish today's short passage.

They have no neighbouring boats, so he takes the opportunity to have a skinny dip. Victoria likes it here and after lunch he rows her into the uninhabited end of the beach where she can explore while being able to see any potential danger from a long way off. There are freshwater showers on the beach so he gives himself a thorough scrubbing.

An easily reached tavern tops a small hill at the western extreme of the bay but their finances mean that meals are always taken aboard these days. Their galley consists of storage racks, a two-ring gas cooker and a cold-water supply - more realistically, an ambient temperature water supply. No grill, no oven, no fridge. He buys those local fruit and vegetables that are bred to survive unsophisticated conditions. Stored carefully the dark leafed Greek lettuce will last a week, locally grown beans the same.

On top of the hill to the south they see vehicles moving silently. Twenty years ago, there would have been traffic noise but now only long-distance trucks and coaches are able to have diesel engines. Small local delivery vans and private cars have been all electric since 2031 though taxis are still using hybrids. It isn't a problem for Victoria and himself in this comparatively isolated spot but walking in town these days requires more care than before.

Sitting in the cockpit later in the afternoon they watch four yachts arrive with the afternoon wind from the west, all crowding in behind the hill with the tavern, all subsequently snubbing away at their anchors. He's learned the hard way to anchor off open terrain if possible. You get the full strength of the wind, but it is more consistent in direction and therefore more likely to dig an anchor in well rather than try to uproot it.

At her stern one of the recently arrived yachts flies the Welsh national flag. He's never sure how to view former countries of the UK. When Wales gained independence, he'd been bemused by the Welsh governments' desire to remove themselves from the clutches of England only to throw in their lot with the EU where they would be even smaller fry. At the time it had seemed to him to be an odd decision but small self-governing regions/countries with loose ties to neighbours were becoming the norm. Loose ties appearing to mean that they would compete with neighbours at times and cooperate with them at others. He understood how this would work in a small comparatively well-ordered world such as sport. For example, football clubs in a league compete with each other regularly but would unite to show combined strength when it came to negotiating with a potential sponsor of the whole league.

However, he had no idea how it could possible work for the complexity which is 30+ EU countries. And the EU itself was only a small part of a planet using up its resources quicker than laying them down … No, he had no answers, the topic was completely beyond him. But he did wonder if in, say, six generations time society would have run out of technological fixes for things and have reverted to more tribal structures. Bad news for multiculturalism and even worse news for ethnic minorities.

'But what do I know?' he said to Victoria, coming back to the tiny world he is able to cope with, usually.

NINE

2019

As arranged, he and Anneke met at the Sea Mice. The weather was certainly in their favour. Sunny with a ten knot southwesterly allowing them to sail on a course a little east of south. Being an old-fashioned yacht, Sandpiper was steady rather than quick so they were overtaken by most of the others heading south from Hoorn that day. Not that this mattered, while he was on the helm Anneke picked her way slowly around deck, familiarising herself with what little the boat had to offer by way of fittings, looking at the curve of the sails on their close reach setting. Something she had been unable to do on the narrow river Yare in Norfolk. She looked happy and he loved her, it seemed completely natural to think that. Later she sat smiling to herself at the helm, steering while he made cheese and salad sandwiches for lunch which they ate in the cockpit, sharing a can of Amstel while Sandpiper sailed on at four knots or so. After lunch they turned and headed back towards the west coast of the Markermeer, anchoring around 4 p.m. as close into the shore as they dared, immediately south of the Marken lighthouse.

'In the mood for swimming?' she asked then teasingly added. 'Skinny dipping, I think you Brits call it.'

'If you are then I'll join you is my assertive reply,' he joked as he unlatched Sandpiper's stern ladder, letting the lower two rungs splash into the water.

There were no other people nearby so they stripped off in the cockpit, openly looking at each other's bodies as they did so. He had never been this close to a fair-haired woman before and the so slight contrast between her curling pubic hair and her lightly tanned body filled him with the desire to bury every part of himself between her legs. Headfirst. His erection was harder than it had ever been, he was certain.

'It looks like you need to cool off,' she said, climbing down the ladder before wincing as her feet found the first rung below water.

It was cold to start with (and the inevitable end of his erection) but they quickly adjusted to the water temperature, circumnavigating the boat in different directions, kissing at the bow and again at the stern.

Paul climbed back on board first and towelled himself dry before Anneke appeared from below and stood dripping in the cockpit, her nipples mirroring his former erection.

'Have you any idea of what a devastating

combination of sexy and lovable you are?' he asked as he sank to his knees in front of her. She did not answer but leaned forward slightly to make it easy for him to take her nipples, in turn, into his mouth, softly kneading and kissing them as his hands slowly and gently roamed over the curves of her wet buttocks. Her smooth skin should have felt cold and clammy but his mind registered only warmth and love.

After a few moments she put her hands on his head, 'Dry me then fuck me,' she commanded.

Later he told her about Sandpiper Rule Number One - on the first night of a cruise the skipper cooks the evening meal. On one gas ring he simmered in olive oil fresh vegetables bought that morning, near the end adding a tin of chilli con carne. On the other ring he boiled rice. They ate in the cockpit watching in the distance the sun gradually lowering over Marken, a pretty village originally populated by Norwegians. They had a second glass of wine as sunset bathed the small lighthouse in warm shades, orange and was that a flash of green? He wondered if he had ever felt as happy as this. They made love again after dark and once more in the morning.

Lazily away in late morning they sailed a little north of east to the other side of the Markermeer and took a marina berth in Leylystad for the night, later wandering around town before eating a rijstaffel for two at an Indonesian restaurant. They were now openly expressing love for each other as on the third day they sailed back to Hoorn. They were not sure how things would work out, but they would be together. He told her he had to sort out something with Ben in four- or five-days' time but he would be back here as soon as possible after that. They parted at the yacht club quay promising to call each other every few days until united once more.

Instead of stopping in Hoorn for the night he sailed back to Marken, anchoring in late evening in the same spot as before. He sat in the cockpit silently affirming his love for Ben, Anneke and his mother. Somehow, he would make a life with them in it. And Gunton and Jan out of it.

In the morning the wind was veering westerly, so it was an easy sail south. In the early afternoon they anchored in the Buiten Ij, just off Durgerdam. Here they were only two miles from the Oranjesluis, the eastern end of Amsterdam, then it would be around four hours along the Noord Zee Canaal to the open sea at Ijmuiden. All being well they should be heading for Harwich tomorrow afternoon. First though, Durgerdam was one of Jan's contact points so he called, receiving a short, 'Ja?' Paul said that they were at anchor among the barges.

'We will visit you during the night. It will be a

short visit then you are free to go back to England. The wind is coming good for that.' The call ended before he could agree about the wind.

He was woken around 1 a.m. by the sound of a boat coming alongside. It was the big man once more. 'We are going to give you greater fuel capacity for your auxiliary engine,' he said, heaving a 22-litre tank onto Sandpiper's deck. It had the correct fittings to be a straight exchange for the boat's usual 10 litre one. The man put the smaller tank in his own boat and connected the larger to Sandpiper's small Johnson auxiliary engine before turning to Paul, 'Do not expect to be able to use the Johnson at all. Is this understood?' he asked.

So, a doctored fuel tank, Paul wondered how much of its 22 litres the consignment occupied then, unpremeditated, answered in Dutch, 'Dat begrijp ik,' (I understand that).

The man smiled in surprise, 'Leuk,' he said, then continued in English. 'You are expected to be at anchor near the houseboats on Oulton Broad in three days. The wind is good to start today.'

It was Paul's turn to be surprised as the big man offered his hand. It was a vice-like grip and Paul steeled himself not to rub his aching hand until the man's dinghy had disappeared into the background gloom.

At first light he checked the weather forecasting app. Forecasts for six- or seven-days' time were a notoriously long way from a guarantee and his original north-easterly had become an easterly veering south-easterly for 30 to 40 hours before a weak front coming through brought the UK east coast a south-westerly. In short, perfect weather for a crossing to Harwich followed by sailing north to return to the Norfolk Broads via Lowestoft. It would look as if he were returning from a typical UK east coast cruise.

He made five packs of sandwiches, filled two flasks with coffee and placed a large bar of chocolate within easy reach of the cockpit. It was just after 8 a.m. when Sandpiper set off under engine towards the Oranjesluis. They had been running for only ten minutes when the engine stuttered, seeming for a few seconds to be firing on only one of its two cylinders. He felt a moment of panic, but the engine returned to its normal smooth running before he could take any action. Had they doctored his main fuel tank as well? Steering with one hand he opened the stern locker with the other and saw that it looked like the usual fuel tank. Filled with dread he cautiously approached the Oranjesluis which opened to allow a small barge and two yachts to exit after which Sandpiper entered the lock as slowly as possible. Above the background noise he heard a burst of vhf radio transmission. Half a minute later a man appeared on the side of the lock urging Paul to tie up immediately inside the gate that allowed access to Amsterdam. He soon saw why as shortly after an enormous barge entered the lock and seemed to occupy at least 95% of it, leaving Sandpiper about half a metre clear of its port bow. If his engine failed now the beast would just crush them on its way out.

But the engine behaved impeccably, and they motored on through Amsterdam. Once heading west Paul found that the wind had veered sufficiently to give them a close then beam reach along the Noord Zee Canaal. Approaching the locks at Ijmuiden he started the engine ready to take the sails down. It ran smoothly for a half a minute then stopped and would not respond to frantic pulling on the starter cord. He gave up and concentrated on sailing into a quay on the south side of the canal, coming alongside with only minor violence. He tied Sandpiper to ship sized bollards below a sign reading Geen Ligplaats (No Mooring).

He removed the engine cowling, found the toolkit and was burning his hand trying to remove a spark plug when two port officials came up, telling him to move. An ocean-going tug was due and will need to moor here. He explained about the engine. The two men conferred before one of them spent what seemed to be many minutes on his mobile while the other motioned Paul to remain where he was. Not that that they could move anyway.

The man with the phone eventually turned to Paul and said that Sandpiper will be towed through the lock to the Seaport Marina where the onsite engineer will look at the engine. That was a much better solution than he'd hoped for and, relieved, he thanked the officials though the back of his mind was calculating that a tow from the marina workboat plus an hour or two of the engineer's time must come to at least 300 Euros, after which he would be pretty much penniless.

A dot in the distance gradually became a police boat. Once he realised it was heading straight for Sandpiper his former relief turned to despair. Christ. His mind was racing, they know. How? His fall was to be a swift one. Donald Crowhurst's words, *it is the mercy*, flashed into his head. Stuck there and helpless he resigned himself to failure as the police boat neared. Ben's father, Anneke's lover, his mother's son, the criminal who would be spending decades in prison. One of life's failures. The police boat slowed as it approached. He could feel that his face was somehow changing shape. If there was a face of guilt then he'd just acquired it.

To his surprise one of the two policemen, the younger one, was smiling as they came alongside and tied up to Sandpiper. 'We will tow you to the marina,' he said, jokingly adding, 'no charge!'

The older policeman was not smiling though. 'Is that small engine on the stern broken also?' he asked. Paul explained that the auxiliary engine just had a neutral and forward gear and was useful only for getting you somewhere near home rather than being any good at manoeuvring the boat in locks or marinas.

His answer was accepted and the police efficiently got them through the lock but during the short tow to the marina Paul relief was shattered as he realised that they had cleverly given him the impression that all would be well just to deal with the Geen Ligplaats problem, they would arrest him when Sandpiper was safely secured in the marina. Then they would have time to take his boat apart looking for whatever it was.

They took him to the far end of the fuel berth where the marina engineer waited. No arrest followed and a grateful Paul shook hands with the policemen, thanking them profusely before they set off back to the lock. He was almost incoherent with relief for a minute or two but must have explained enough to the engineer who quickly established that it was the small unit which controlled the timing of the spark which had failed. In the workshop he had an older version of the same engine which he cannibalised, fitting its controller to Sandpiper's engine which then started first time and ran sweetly for a five-minute trial. Thank heavens. While the controller was being changed, he could see marina staff leaving for the night so the engineer had worked into overtime. This is going to be expensive thought Paul as he asked how much he owed. 'Oh, 60 Euros,' the man replied. If cats have nine lives each then Paul knew he'd already pushed his luck well beyond two cats' worth. He pressed 80 Euros into the man's hand and the engineer left after another grateful handshake.

A few minutes later Sandpiper slipped her mooring and motored out of the marina. He hoisted full sail in the outer harbour and started for Harwich, some 120 miles of North Sea away. Their lucky streak continued as the southeast to east wind of 12 to 15 knots held and twenty-six hours later Sandpiper passed the Pye End buoy and headed southwest along the narrow-buoyed channel into the Walton Backwaters, just east of Harwich. Half an hour later they anchored in Hamford Water. He would have loved to stay here for some days, venturing further into Landermere Creek, the setting for Arthur Ransome's book, Secret Waters, but he now had less than 24 hours to make it back to the Broads. Ben must be coming up to the age when he'd appreciate Arthur Ransome's stories and he'd been looking forward to reading his son The Coot Club, a tale set in the Broads area. He cooked a quick meal from cans, set the alarm for early morning and crashed out.

He awoke to a feeling of sadness. It was while making

toast that he realised the sadness was due to the fact that, if Plan A was his future, he had just spent his last night in this premier division sailing area. There were few places as good for a sailor as the Essex and Suffolk rivers and coast.

In the past he had made a habit of talking to his favourite navigational aids as he passed them and as Sandpiper sailed close to the Pye End buoy he said goodbye to his old friend whose rusting red and white stripes did nothing to lift his sadness. On her northeast course Sandpiper sailed on, the coastal tidal flow becoming favourable as they passed the mouth of the Deben. The advantageous tide quickened, and they sailed at six to seven knots past the pagodas on Orfordness where atomic tests were carried out in Word War 2. They were making eight knots as the tide squeezed them past the Orfordness Lighthouse, now out of commission but still proudly erect, defying the encroaching sea. Coastal erosion would mean the end for the lighthouse in a few years and he suddenly burst into tears as he said goodbye to his old friend. Once in the past he had anchored here in a flat calm, waiting for wind. Other times he had battered his way past in horrible wind against tide seas. It was comparatively gentle today, a worthy end to a relationship. Another twenty minutes and Aldeburgh was abeam. Picked out in the morning sun this handsome town had always been a heartening sight for him and so it was that day.

There was a weak phone signal and he managed to establish that there would be bridge and lock openings at 3.30 p.m., and there was room for Sandpiper. This would get them from Lowestoft's inner harbour into Oulton Broad. He also knew that there would be a scheduled 2.30 p.m. opening of the bridge connecting Lowestoft's outer to inner harbours and, at their current pace, they would be in plenty of time for that.

So it proved, he berthed Sandpiper to the pontoon in the trawl dock for forty minutes until called for the 2.30 bridge opening. All went smoothly and an hour later they joined one other boat in Mutford Lock. Paul paid the £15 fee thinking that for this payment the yacht station staff had to open one railway bridge, one road bridge, one footbridge and one lock, all in a sequence which minimised disruption to road traffic. Could there be better value? Out of the lock, elation mounting, he motored Sandpiper for ten minutes before anchoring at the quiet end of the broad, near the houseboats. 'Done it!' he shouted, scaring many nearby birds into flight.

Having wound down a little he made himself a pot of tea and ate the last pack of sandwiches made at anchor off Durgerdam just yesterday morning though it seemed long ago. He phoned the contact number which was answered by Jan who congratulated him and said that he would be visited between 1 and 2 a.m.

Too tired and tense to sleep he decided to sit inside the cabin to await the small hours visit. It was clear that he was now completely vulnerable. Together Gunton and Jan could overpower him, shackle two or three metres of chain around his middle and tip him overboard to his death. The nautical equivalent of that old Mafia classic, the concrete overcoat, where the body of an undesirable would be included in a building's foundations. The water here was murky, his body would never be found until some unlucky boat owner snagged him with their anchor, or an angler had a particularly bad day. Gunton and Jan would leave Sandpiper there at anchor, a mystery. Eventually someone would make the link to his interest in Donald Crowhurst, he'd talked about this to a couple of colleagues and it might be assumed that he'd followed Crowhurst, fifty years on. The consignment would be in the hands of Gunton and Jan and they would not have to pay the transportation fee.

'Paul.' He awoke with a start to see a man framed between himself and the cockpit. Jan? Gunton? Paul's mouth had an acidic taste and his neck ached from falling asleep sitting up.

'It's OK,' said Jan, 'you have done well, we will take our goods and then pay you.'

Paul stood watching Gunton and Jan who had arrived silently alongside in a large rib with an electric engine. From their boat they took a 4hp Johnson outboard engine, identical to Sandpiper's auxiliary, and exchanged it with the one on his boat's stern. 'This one works,' said Gunton. Even in this low light Paul could see the bastard's smirk.

They also exchanged fuel tanks so Sandpiper no longer had an oversize one. Paul thought that this 4hp engine that had crossed the North Sea with them could be regarded as either useless (as an engine) or very valuable (for what it contained). He wondered if the engine-which-wasn't-an-engine looked like a normal one inside its cowling. And had they filled its insides with packs of white powder? He knew the names of various drugs of course but wasn't going to say them in his mind. Well, he'd never know now, and he was certainly not going to ask.

Jan turned towards him. 'In this envelope you will find two hundred fifty-pound notes. You are suspicious of course but you will find that they are real currency.' He waited assuming Paul would open the envelope to check. When he didn't, Jan continued, 'You will also make one more run then your son, Ben, will be safe and you can go wherever you want. Same payment as this,' he pointed to the envelope. A continuing threat, Paul could think of nothing to say that would be appropriate in his current position so remained sitting in the cabin.

'Relax for a week then we will make contact. Again, you did well,' said Jan. They left, heading towards the north shore of the Broad. He continued sitting, numb and disconnected. It was not until some minutes later that he reached for the envelope which did indeed contain two hundred pieces of papery material which looked like fifty-pound notes, though he could hardly claim close acquaintance with ones that large. The criminal had been paid for his crime.

He slept fitfully until mid-morning then set off for his mooring at Davison's Dyke, arriving just before dark. Not bothering to eat he climbed into the sleeping bag and was dead to the world for over eleven hours.

The day following his return from Holland he remained very tired and achieved little apart from phoning Debbie who agreed to a beach day for himself and Ben tomorrow. She mentioned that he needed to keep a couple of hours clear tomorrow evening. 'There's something we need to discuss; we'll have a glass of wine and talk. And I can't say more at the moment as there are one or two things I need to clear during the day,' she added

'Does it relate to access?' he persisted.

'Paul, we'll open a bottle of wine tomorrow and discuss things in a civilised atmosphere,' she said and ended the call leaving him to a worrying evening running through what the discussion would be about. Had his acting in the Debbie Standard Father role been inadequate? It must surely have something to do with access. And also with MGBman? About whom he'd avoided researching, possibly fearing what he might find. Was Debbie moving? It had to be something major to warrant the phrase 'discuss things in a civilised atmosphere'. The one certainty was that there would be change and he would lose by it.

Resignedly he assembled Ben's bag for tomorrow - bucket, spade, high factor sun cream etc. He expected to be too worked up to sleep but set the alarm for 8 a.m. as a protection. He called Anneke whose phone went unanswered again. He texted to say that they were back on the dyke mooring, all OK and looking forward to hearing from her.

To his surprise he slept well and was woken by the alarm. He cycled to Ben's home where the MGB stood in the drive. Clearly, its owner was openly staying overnight now. Debbie opened the door and Ben rushed out to hug his father's legs before he could bend down to kiss him. He looked at Debbie who showed the vertical palm of her hand and mouthed, 'this evening.'

On the train to Great Yarmouth Ben was full of questions about his sail to Holland. How fast did

Sandpiper sail? Were the people nice? Taking an opportunity to introduce the idea of Anneke he mentioned meeting a friend in Hoorn where there were statues of the sea mice, saying also why they were there. Ben immediately fell for the sea mice (it was the name he supposed) and wanted to meet them! Paul had to explain that statues were representations of people and things we should remember. They were made of very hard and strong materials like metal and stone so they would last a very long time.

'Strong bond stone,' said Ben immediately, smiling broadly, impressing his father with his brain power yet again. What could this boy become?

Paul managed to stop himself saying that statues would usually outlive the humans they represented. Ben didn't need to learn about his mortality just yet. Thinking that his son's continuing interest in the sea mice came perhaps from their size, he explained that while children like Ben grow in size as they get older the sea mice will always be the same as they are now. They must stay the same size because they were designed to represent the children stolen to work on boats in the South Sea.

'Will I be a sea mouse one day?' Ben asked.

'Only if I steal you and rush off carrying you under my arm then sail away never to be seen again,' he answered. Ben laughed and mimed carrying James

191

(his teddy bear) off. If only he knew.

Later, Ben was happily building sandcastles when he asked if there were beaches in Sweden.

'Sweden? Yes, I expect so, but I've never been there. Why do you ask?'

Ben looked uncomfortable as he realised that his father did not know. 'Scott going to work in Sweden,' he said.

Scott? MGBman? 'The man with the MGB car?'

'Yes. Mummy and Ben going with him,' said the small boy, looking tearful now, seeing from his father's reaction that he'd said something wrong.

Paul's mind was whirling and something acidic was corroding his stomach, but he mostly responded to his son's tearful face, cuddling him and saying that Daddy will always love him more than anything in the world no matter where they both were. Even if Ben was in Sweden. 'Even if you were a sea mouse working in the South Sea,' he said with a smile.

After a few minutes of being reassured by his father, Ben went back to his castles leaving Paul to face his worst fear, the loss of his son. MGBman (he couldn't bring himself to call him Scott) was going to work in Sweden and thought Debbie and Ben would go with him. That was their plan, but Paul knew now that theirs was going to be upstaged by his own. Plan A would operate first, Ben was going to join the sea mice much earlier than he thought.

The MGB was still there when they arrived back. Debbie opened the door and Ben rushed into the house as usual.

'Sweden?' said Paul, quietly so Ben would not hear.

'Come back at 8 p.m. when Ben's gone down,' she replied in kind as the door shut.

Having nearly three hours to kill he thought of going to the pub for something to eat then decided against it - it would mean breaking into the first ill-gotten fifty-pound note, a large note that the landlord might remember. Instead he returned to Sandpiper and sat uselessly rehashing all yesterday's thoughts.

At almost exactly 8 p.m. he walked past the MGB and knocked on the door which was answered by Debbie. He followed her into the lounge where a man stood and came towards him. Perhaps two inches shorter than himself but stockier. Broad shoulders and black curly hair framed a wide, dark complexioned face. A magnet for women seeking the gypsy type.

'Hello I'm Scott Benfield,' he said in his deep voice, offering his hand.

Paul indulged the man with the shortest possible handshake and said, 'And I'm Paul Williams,' then added after a slight delay, 'Ben's father.'

'Yes, I did know that,' the man said, half smiling,

'But I didn't know if you knew who I was.'

Standing close, looking at each other made Paul think that this could go beyond verbal sparring and he'd had no physical confrontation since that fight with Bonner at school, was it in year three? Whatever, he wasn't going to soften his tone. 'Why would I know, to me you are just MGBman, a person whose car is here frequently,' he said, continuing to look straight into the man's face ignoring Debbie who was trying to usher him into a seat with a glass of wine on a table in front of it.

'When you left ClanCo I was recruited to take your place in the Planning Department, I started a month after you left,' said Benfield.

Astonished, Paul sat as directed. The other two followed suit, watching carefully for his reaction. The bloody man had his job, his wife and his son and now sat in the role of host in the house Paul was paying for. Benfield the Conqueror. The winner. The main man.

After a sip of wine Debbie broke the silence, 'Scott has been head-hunted for the job of Chief Planning Engineer at the main Volvo factory near Gothenburg. In Sweden,' she added. Then, undeterred by Paul's ironically raised eyebrow she continued. 'Scott starts there on September the first. We will be married here at the city hall in two weeks and will live on the outskirts of Gothenburg where, to start with, we have rented a house. I know it's short notice and I'm sorry it's a shock but we only firmed things up recently, when you had just left for Holland. And this conversation had to be face to face.' She sat back in her chair and gulped at her wine, clearly nervous.

Paul asked her, 'And Ben, the only person I care about, the centre of my life. He remains unmentioned so far.' He had not intended to be that sarcastic but wasn't about to start apologising now.

It was Benfield who answered, 'As you know, toward the end of a job interview they always ask if you have questions for them. I said I would be married shortly and that my wife-to-be had a four-year-old son with a very high IQ. Was there a school in Gothenburg suitable for him? They said they would be surprised if there were not, but they would get back to me on that. I had a call two days later. There is an excellent school and they have booked a provisional place for him. Acceptance will depend on a test but I'm sure Ben will fly through it.'

Paul thought this bastard's been planning Ben's future in Sweden while I was planning Ben's future on the high seas.

He must have looked stunned; Debbie wore a worried expression as she continued to try to sell him her vision of Ben's future in Sweden. 'Gothenburg University has a good reputation too. Ben is going to get the stretching he needs.'

Having said the words they must have practised,

they looked at each other, then at Paul, who looked at Benfield. 'You plan the future of my son.'

'He's my son too,' said Debbie softly.

'I will make sure his intellect is stretched, it's what Ben deserves, and I know that this is what you want. Your reputation at ClanCo is still high,' said Benfield. An answer he'd clearly thought through beforehand.

Debbie continued, 'Access will be more difficult, obviously, but we will be helpful. There are cheap flights. Ryanair fly Stansted to Gothenburg. Norwegian Airways and BA also fly there. I can book you into a nearby guest house for a couple of nights. Although you'll see Ben less frequently it will be for longer periods.'

Paul sat in silence, trying to imagine himself in this man with a suitcase mode. Debbie wondered if he'd retreated into his own world again, surely not, this was Ben's future they were discussing.

Eventually Paul asked, 'What do you expect me to say? This is a fait accompli, I have no decisions to make.'

Debbie replied, 'The purpose of this evening is to show you that none of this is to spite you. It's a career move that Scott can't refuse and I am going with him as his wife. We are both obviously concerned that this will hurt you deeply and we are trying to reassure you that Ben is priority number one. I know you have been worried that the local village school here won't provide what he needs.'

She looked at Benfield who quietly said, 'Financial.'

'Yes,' said Debbie, then, turning to Paul, she continued. 'Without the expense of solicitors, I hope we can come to an agreement regarding the house and Ben's maintenance payments. My suggestions are these ...

One: We put the house up for sale right away and whatever money is left over after the mortgage is settled, and selling fees paid, you and I will split 50-50 between us.

Two: From the end of this month and continuing until the house is sold, I will transfer half of the mortgage payment into your account. In other words, we pay equally for the house until it is sold.

Three: The monthly payment you make for Ben's maintenance ceases at the end of this month after which this responsibility will be mine and Scott's.'

'You will be much better off financially,' she said finally.

'But not in any other way,' Paul quickly responded.

'You'll have enough to start again, a flat in the city perhaps,' she said.

'And all I lose is a son.'

'No, not lost, just further away and being well cared for. It's not a bereavement, Paul.'

'How has Ben taken this?'

'He knows he won't see you so often, but he and

Scott get on very well with each other. Ben is at an age when he can adapt, and he will have plenty to do to pick up the language. Though this should be straightforward as almost all Swedes under seventy speak English as a second language. Even so, Volvo have engaged a linguist to give us Swedish lessons on two evenings a week. We will work at it; we are going to integrate quickly.'

Paul sat in silence. Debbie finished her wine and continued, 'Come back on Saturday at 6 p.m. and have tea with the three of us. You can put Ben to bed. Seeing the people who love and care for him all together will do wonders for his current and future well-being. Oh, and please think about my financial proposals,' she added.

Paul nodded and stood up, thoughts cycling incoherently, wine untouched.

Benfield stood also and approached, 'This has been a dreadful shock for you, and I am genuinely sorry for that. I wish we could meet on other than this basis. Please believe me, I will look after him.'

The man looked sincere, Paul nodded and turned for the door.

Sleep finally arrived sometime after 3 a.m. Before then his mind would not settle to coherent thought. It flickered around dealing only with incidental, trivial things such as names. Benfield was just a year or two younger than him but somehow seemed more modern, more of this age. Was it just his name? A little over one hundred years ago in World War 1, pals regiments were filling up with men with names like Paul Williams. There would have been no Scott Benfields.

Ben Benfield, BenBen, TwoBen. Was a name like Ben Benfield an asset or a liability? He laughed at himself, realising that he'd absorbed accountant speak. He vaguely remembered stage or celebrity names he'd heard that he'd thought silly at the time (Sloop Dog? Orangey Sprocket?) but which didn't seem to have been a handicap. Benfield had replaced him as an engineer, a husband and now as a father. Nothing important then.

He awoke with a dry mouth, a dull headache and the awful knowledge that Ben was being taken away from him.

What a mismatch of time - if only Gunton and Jan had approached him this morning he could have refused or, at least, played for time because, by the end of the month, Ben would be safely in Gothenburg and, surely, their tentacles would not reach that far?

His phone showed no text from Anneke. He called but it was unanswered once more. Clearly, there was something wrong here too. He decided to catch a bus into the city to buy a cheap mobile phone, put a minimum top up on it and try her number again on the assumption that her screen would not recognise the number as his. In the nearest shop to the bus station he used two of his criminally 'earned' fifty-pound notes to buy a phone and try again, realising as he did that her screen would still show the UK dial code. It was unanswered too but at least the move showed that the fifties were real currency.

Back on Sandpiper he decided that as it was only Thursday he could have a couple of nights on Eastland Broad. A second weekend of reckoning. And it didn't matter a damn that it was not the weekend.

They motored to Ferry Stores where he topped up Sandpiper's water containers and bought two large bars of chocolate, a family sized pack of crisps and two bottles of wine. Comfort food. A long way from his usual basic foodstuffs.

'What's the celebration, Paul?' asked Jenny, the store owner.

'It's the other way round,' he answered lightly, 'I trying to find something to celebrate and think that by buying these something to celebrate will come along and find me.'

He'd been coming to the store twice a week for a couple of years now, so they were familiar enough with each other for the occasional bantering. Jenny pointed to the bottle of Carmenere. 'That's one of my favourites so if you're looking for someone to celebrate with then I'm your girl. Well, apart from having to run the store for twelve hours a day, look after three kids and a dog. Oh, and a husband.'

'Well, if it wasn't for that lot, I'd capture you for a naughty weekend on the boat. You know, club yer over the 'ead caveman style and drag yer away,' he replied, turning for the door.

She laughed, 'You won't need the club.'

With less than three miles to the broad he decided to use the engine only. Usually he was alert to Sandpiper's natural surroundings, keeping an eye open for any floating 'gifts' lost from hireboats - boathooks, fenders etc. Most of Sandpiper's motley collection of fenders had arrived by this route but today he was thinking of the exchange with Jenny. He was easily able to play roles which demanded the sort of performance he'd given in the store. And, despite that one recent disintegrating class, he could usually play the role of teacher reasonably well. But what of the role of father? Was he just playing the role of loving, caring father on access day?

Was he asking if there was more to a father-son bond than the playing of a set role? The world contained an awful lot of fathers and sons, more than enough to establish a typical pattern of behaviour from which small deviations in the role playing of father were to be expected. Then he realised he was walking around the killer question. Is Benfield going to be a better father for Ben than I will be? The unavoidable question.

TEN

2039:

Palioumilou to Vonitsa & Ay Markou

He usually thinks of the light early morning north-easterly wind as the gentle breath of the mountains whose grey outline can be seen to the north of the gulf. Unfortunately, the mountain's breath doesn't reach as far as Palioumilou so if he wishes to sail rather than motor (and he does) then they must tack against the much stronger afternoon westerly.

In late morning they motor quietly past the fish farm and raise full sail to drift for thirty minutes until the afternoon wind establishes and they start to make progress. In three hours, the wind is up to 24 to 30 knots over the deck and they are double reefed and pitching in the short, sharp chop. As usual Victoria lies low in the cabin, at the minimum motion point. He gains a little by taking advantage of the wind curling around the western headland of Ormos

Rougas but it's another hour before their motion changes to a more gentle rolling as they beam reach south into the small bay at the eastern end of Vonitsa. The bay is formed by high ground to the east and a small uninhabited island to the west, joined to the mainland by a pedestrian width causeway. Here there's good protection from everything but a northerly. There are another seven or eight boats at anchor in the bay.

Vonitsa is a small town and, in common with much of the urban life of southern Europe these days, packs of dogs roam the streets. This eastern end of town is the territory of the pack he calls the Huskies, named after their leader, a large grey and white brute who probably isn't a husky but looks strong enough to pull a laden sled on his own. Today, needing to get to a cash machine he's rowed into the mainland end of the causeway and is walking to the town centre when Husky and his seven strong pack round a corner and lope towards him, inducing the now familiar-in-this-situation feeling of helplessness. And fear, he is not a dog person. Luckily, they ignore him and are obviously heading for the beach along with what seems to be a potential new pack member. A thin medium sized brown mongrel is trotting hopefully along two or three metres behind the closely grouped others. A fringe dog. Passing the beach a little later he sees the pack sitting or lying on the beach, apparently happy, facing the water like the family groups of surrounding humans, the fringe dog a short distance behind them and ignored by the pack.

It amuses him that the dogs are copying human beach behaviour but his negative side wonders what happens when the living gets more difficult, as it surely must soon. Humans are particularly vulnerable here, wearing little and being so easily outrun and brought down by a pack of dogs. Carrying a firearm is still illegal in Greece and if a human were set upon it is almost certain that neighbouring humans would make for safety rather than try to help. It must be impossible to fight off eight hungry dogs, he thought, and it would be a very painful death as your flesh is torn away. He wondered how big an evolutionary step it would be for the fringe dog to work out that one possible way to make his mark with the pack would be to savage a nearby child, many of whom were almost advertising themselves in their nakedness. You are a pessimist he said to himself as he turned and looked again at the pack, seeming to enjoy doing what the humans do. It's a scene that would make most people smile but he can't help thinking that one day the pack will be more hungry than usual, something will spook them and ...

Over the years he's been in Vonitsa many times and knows where to buy the cheap locally concocted and unlabelled ouzo - bring your own bottle and save even more. He treats himself today and that evening sits in the cockpit with a glass watching the sun set over the crumbling Venetian fort on the top of a hill to the west of the town. The fort's details are better seen picked out in the morning sun as it appears over the high ground to the east, but the time for an ouzo is now. And tonight, he decides, is a night for a second glass. He looks across at Victoria, sees her in profile and is overcome by a feeling of love and tenderness. A feeling heightened by his earlier thoughts. If she is attacked by a pack of dogs then he will launch himself into them and die alongside her.

Two mornings later they motor the two miles across the bay and anchor in Ay Markou, its horseshoe shape giving maximum protection from the swell caused by the afternoon wind. Its downside is its depth, the sounder reading 13 metres as he lowers the anchor and all of the 40 metres of chain the boat has. It's Saturday tomorrow and he wants to be in Preveza by late morning so everything he's lowered will have to be heaved up again before first light, a good ten minutes work at his age. Worth it though, this is his special place.

Most of Ay Markou's shoreline is densely planted but there's an open space at the northeast corner of the anchorage and he rows Victoria over for some land time in the afternoon. Later, in the early evening they sit in the cockpit watching a mixed flock of sheep and goats pick their slow way through the open space, heading for their night quarters.

'Oi,' the old goatherd shouts as he recognises their boat.

'Oi,' he replies in return. They've been seeing each other this way for fifteen years or so, the same vocal exchange each time. Oi, no more is needed to express friendly recognition.

When he first arrived in the Preveza region, he'd spent seven weeks at anchor here in Ay Markou, having realised that this was the first area for a long time in which he felt comfortable. He decided that it would be the base for the rest of his life, a decision he's never regretted. From here the three-mile round trip by rowing boat to buy supplies in Vonitsa had been a necessary hardship. A necessary step in the move away from his previously nomadic life in the Mediterranean. And, apart from 'Oi's, this shopping formed his only human contact during those seven weeks.

ELEVEN

2019

He anchored in the same place as before for his not-the-weekend of reckoning. It was nearly 6 p.m. He opened the Carmenere, poured himself a glass and turned on the radio. The prime minister was considering the dissolving of parliament and Paul thought about what, if he had the PM's power, he would dissolve. In the current situation the dissolving or disappearing of himself would simplify everything for Debbie and Benfield. He poured another glass, perhaps that was the answer. Paulexit. No deal needed any more. No deal the best outcome.

The Archers theme tune came on and he fumbled for the radio's off button. Maudlin, now there was a role he was straight from central casting for. He poured a third glass. He's losing Ben and his senses tell him he's losing Anneke too. He's a loser. Hail Benfield the Conqueror.

He awoke around 9 a.m., the thick tongued owner of another dull headache. Only the stupid drink themselves senseless on their boat. Only the truly stupid do so when they are singlehanded and at anchor. Stupid, there's another apt role.

Around mid-morning, after a third mug of coffee, he felt able to focus on what action he should take. In many ways the situation was straightforward. At the end of the month, just twenty-one days away, Ben would move to Sweden. The only way he could stop this was to snatch Ben and sail off, Plan A. He didn't have it in great detail yet, but he'd done enough research to know that it was feasible. If Plan A was the choice, then he'd have to buy their escape yacht in the Portsmouth area within the next few days. Given the timescale it would have to be pretty much ready for long distance sailing when it was bought. Ideally, it would just need provisioning. And it would have to cost less than five thousand pounds, leaving them around the same amount to start their new life. An amount which seemed very thin, but he'd had plenty of practice at economical living.

If he shelves Plan A then what life choices does he have? One of those how long is a piece of string questions. He could do whatever he liked, all that kept him here was Ben. He would not be able to follow his son, the chance of getting a teaching job in the Gothenburg area was close to zero. He wasn't qualified to teach English and, even if he was, to do so he'd have to speak excellent Swedish as a first language. No chance there. His life would have to be other than in Sweden. He really needed to know if Anneke and himself had a future together. He wrote her one more text message ...

Dear Anneke. I haven't heard from you and fear the worst. I've just learned that the situation with Ben is to change drastically. I can't decide anything until I know how we stand. I hope but am fearful. Your loving Paul.

He forced himself to think through the option of staying here, living as Debbie thought he would, judging by what she said yesterday. That is, continuing at the college, flying to Gothenburg on the occasional weekend plus the same in the college holidays, eventually buying a small flat in the city where Ben could visit and stay sometimes, if he wanted to. Despite his visits to Gothenburg being infrequent there would come a time when something Ben wanted to do, or the family Benfield wanted to do, would have to be cancelled because it was a father weekend. Resentment would inevitably grow. Or flights would have to be changed at some expense ... it would only work in the long term if he were living nearby and able to be flexible about access. And who would want to employ him in Gothenburg? On a whim he typed *jobs in sweden for english speakers* into

Google and was surprised to find a few though none were suitable and, all but one, a long way from Gothenburg. No, that was not the answer. He had a sudden vision of applying to Volvo for a job as one of Benfield's planning engineers - bringing about the completion of his journey to the bottom. He'd die first. No, Sweden was unlikely to be short of any skills that he could offer. And staying here and continuing at college as Debbie envisaged was not an option he would take either. Paul had a vision of himself staying here, Benless, growing older, sadder and unfulfilled. Mr Hollow. Mr One Dimensional Man.

Hang on though, what if there was an innocent reason why Anneke had not been answering calls or returning texts, could he stay here if they had a future together? He supposed it was possible, they were both in their thirties, possibly they might start a family. He really did need to hear from her and picked up his phone for one last try at contact. The screen indicated an unread email. He clicked on it.

Dear Paul

I am sorry I have not answered until now. I wanted time to think about my future. When I arrived back in Hoorn at the end of the college term, I found a letter from Frenkie (I mentioned him when you and I were finding out about each other) the fellow student I met at University and had a long term relationship with which ended last year. In his letter he pleaded for a second chance. Despite my growing feelings for you I went to him for a few days then and have been with him again last week. There is no avoiding the fact that I love you both and that I have been selfishly keeping my options open. I can do so no longer and I will stay here in Amsterdam with Frenkie. I have emailed the college to say I am not returning. I will look for a job here. I know that when I am old, I will look back on our few days aboard Sandpiper on the Markermeer as one of the highlights of my life, and I will wonder what sort of life we may have had together. Please believe me when I write that my decision is no reflection on you. You are absolutely lovable and my mother in particular thinks I am an idiot. I do love you so much, but I am weak and, in many ways, unadventurous so I have decided to remain with the man I know best. Please let me know you have received this email and that you accept my decision, hurtful though it may be.

Anneke

He read it twice then sat back in the cockpit, the sudden movement attracting the attention of a couple of ducks which then made for Sandpiper in the hope of something edible. He read the email a third time. It wasn't the bombshell it might have been, Anneke's silence up to this point had already established in his mind first the possibility then the likelihood of rejection. As Dear Johns went it was a very kind one, he supposed. He would have to reply in the same vein. As far as his options were concerned the email put an end to any thought of staying here. In fact, he'd been stupid to think that it was a viable option, Gunton was already pressing him for the start date of the second 'run' and if he completed that successfully they would soon find something else they wanted from him. 'No, the option of Staying Here stops here,' he said to the ducks, who came closer in anticipation only to be told that Paul Williams would sail over the horizon soon. He concentrated on Anneke, made a few notes then selected the email app.

Dear Anneke

Not having heard from you I had begun to fear the worst and now I know it has arrived. Not only have I lost you, the person I thought would be the love of my life, but I am also about to (in effect) lose my son, Ben. His mother is to marry a man who will be taking up a job in Sweden next month. She and Ben will go with him. So, I too will not be returning to college. I have decided to sail off to the south, to wherever the wind takes Sandpiper. Become the wanderer, a role which has always attracted me. On that score perhaps your decision is a sensible one. I realise we will not contact each other again so I would like you to know that you are not weak and unadventurous. At college I admired you before I loved you. You stood out as an upright, honest and utterly wholesome woman, an absolute pleasure to be with. And then I fell for you and discovered that the rest of you was even better! Please never undervalue yourself.

I will always love you but will seek you no longer. Have a good life.

Paul

'And now the big decision,' he said to the two ducks who still hadn't given up hope that food might follow words. Did he concede that Ben's future would be best served by moving to Sweden with Debbie and Benfield? If he did concede this then he'd sail away alone to wherever. He'd call that Plan B. Or did he think Ben would have a better future sailing off with his father, a snatched child to put it baldly, a sea mouse to put it more poetically. That was the now well-established Plan A.

Anyone with half a gram of sense would say choose Plan B, Ben with mother and well-paid stepfather in Sweden while the criminal father sailed off to start a new life where he can't infect Family Benfield. But of course, this mythical person with at least half of a gram of sense would not be in Paul's current position. It was then that he realised the decision did not have to be made that day, as long as he played his hand in the right sequence then he had ten or twelve days in which to do more research on safe destinations. He made notes on the necessary sequence.

Access to Ben had to continue as is, so on Saturday teatime he had to perform the role of a person who'd accepted the situation and who would stay here teaching at college as Debbie and Benfield envisaged.

The college think he'll be returning in September refreshed from the long summer break. He won't but it was necessary to give the impression he would be though he felt guilty about not giving notice. When he didn't turn up there'd be some panic rescheduling, but it would be good for them in the long run in that they'd replace him with a proper teacher, one who owned a suit and looked the part. In short, he'd do whatever it takes to make people think he's staying on at college.

Gunton and Jan think he will be away on the second Holland 'run' within the next few days so next week he'd move Sandpiper to Lowestoft to give them the impression he'd left. He'd catch the train from Lowestoft to the village to pick up Ben on access day. It meant living his final few days in the UK in Lowestoft, but so be it.

If it was to be Plan A then he had to identify and view a suitable small yacht, one that was capable of transporting Ben and himself across an ocean. If Plan B then another yacht would not be necessary - if

Sandpiper foundered with just himself aboard then, again, so be it. So, Plan A - he needed to start a yacht search now, view the yacht as soon as possible, negotiate a price then tell the current owner that he needed a few days to think it over. This would annoy the current owner, but it was a buyer's market at the moment, so he'd have to accept it.

It was going to be an action packed ten days or so. He charged the mobile while he made dinner, finishing off the first bottle of wine as he cooked. Serious yacht search started an hour later. Limiting himself to the Solent area he soon found a Tamar 24 in Gosport on the west side of Portsmouth harbour. At only 24 feet by 8 she was small but Tamars were tough little yachts with a deep, safe centre cockpit and cabins fore and aft. Ben could have his own cabin eventually, an important space for a growing boy. The Tamar was ketch rigged with all sail controls leading into the cockpit. In bad weather offshore three small sails with their controls in the cockpit gave plenty of reefing options. There was also a zip-up cockpit enclosure and an autopilot. The engine had been replaced five years earlier and was now a Kubota based one for which he knew spares were available worldwide. The boat sounded ideal and the photographs showed she was in good condition. He was sure he could negotiate the asking price of £5,500 down to £5,000 or less. He phoned her current owner and arranged a viewing on Monday.

Things were on the move, he poured another glass of wine and looked at the Tamar's photos again. He couldn't see the boat's name but noticed that a neighbouring boat was called Briony. Ha, if he managed to wangle an invitation to board the neighbouring boat then he'd be able to say he'd been inside Briony. 'Williams the Unworthy rears his head again,' he said to the broad in general, now collecting its evening's worth flock of gulls. He smiled, recalling his gorgeous but poisonous ex-student. Silently he again wished his unforgettable beauty well.

His phone rang, Anneke changing her mind? No, Jan wanting a meeting at the pub on Sunday evening. Gunton was away for a few days he said so he would like to meet to talk over a few things, could Paul make 8 p.m.? Oh, and bring the chart folio so others in the pub will think we will be discussing another Holland cruise. Paul agreed to meet at 8 p.m. What did Jan want to talk about with Gunton absent? There would not be an answer to that until Sunday.

On Saturday morning he motored Sandpiper back to her mooring in Davison's Dyke. There he trawled the National Express website and worked up a schedule which allowed a couple of hours to view the Tamar in Gosport on Monday afternoon before starting the return journey. It would be a very early start and a late return. He would be knackered on Tuesday, successfully so he hoped. He caught a bus into the city and bought Monday's national Express tickets at the bus station. Back on Sandpiper he had time to wash and make himself presentable, or what passed for that these days.

At 6 p.m. Ben opened the door, 'Daddy!' he shouted and hugged his father's legs. Paul was eventually able to bend down and kiss his son's head. His lovely boy, so happy to see his father, so determined to take him to his room to show him what he and Scott were working on. Paul barely had time to nod to Debbie and briefly shake hands with Benfield before being led upstairs. Pride of place in Ben's room was a low table full to overflowing with Lego Technic parts. Ben picked up a box built of Lego with three inter-meshing gear wheels on the outside, the smallest of which had a mark on one of its teeth. Ben showed his father how one full revolution of the small wheel produced one sixth of a revolution of the largest. 'Ratio of number of teeth', the boy said proudly.

Christ, some four-year-olds would only just be discovering that they could lock one bit of basic Lego onto another. 'Yes, that's right, Ben, the number of teeth tell you the gear ratio. Did Scott show you this?' he asked.

'Yes, ratio needed for snow plough,' Ben pointed to another part-built model on the table.

Snow plough, Sweden, in their heads they must be there already. And Benfield is putting in quality time with Ben. This is what they wanted to show him by today's invitation. They were showing that Ben would be happy and cared for in Family Benfield. Paul's role today was to show that he accepted this. Well, that's a role he could play. Ben was starting to show him another project when, in an authoritative voice his mother shouted up the stairs, 'Ben, teatime, now.'

A square table had been set with a chair on each side. Clever of them he thought, no head of table place with which to indicate his now subservient place in the household. Paul played his role by talking to Benfield about ClanCo. On handing in his notice Benfield had been given half of an hour to clear his desk before being escorted off the premises by two security men. Evidently there had been nothing nasty about it, he had been put on gardening leave on full pay because the Marketing Department's Venn diagram showed that the newly designed but not yet built ClanCo car had a tiny overlap with the smallest of the current Volvo range. 'Can't see it myself but you know what Marketing's like,' said Benfield and they exchanged a grin, a brief moment of solidarity in the typical engineer's view of stuff coming out of Marketing.

Paul put his son to bed and read him the story Ben selected, Roger and the Elephant, though Woger was closer to his son's pronunciation. How bizarre he thought, this little boy of considerable technical ability should be entranced by such a slight story about a naughty elephant. Or was his pleasure derived from the wholehearted attention of a loved adult?

Downstairs Debbie had opened a bottle of Chilean Carmenere. Jenny's favourite, he smiled at the memory as he sat in the same chair as before. This time he picked up his glass and raised it to them. 'OK, here's to success in all aspects of your life in Sweden. I'm not going to fight. I'll make sure that Ben sees no bitterness in his father's attitude to your moving. I'll leave him with the impression that Sweden will be a wonderful opportunity to live a fulfilling life. I'll make sure that he knows I will always love him and that, when he's older, I will be absolutely delighted to see him. End of speech,' he added, smiling and raising his glass.

'Thank you, Paul. Thank you. You have no idea how worried I've been about how you would take the news.' Taking a large gulp of wine, Debbie sat back in evident relief.

Benfield raised his still full glass. 'And here's to you, Paul. A man whose work I've admired at ClanCo and now a man whose attitude I admire even more. To you,' Benfield drank from his glass. He seemed sincere.

Nodding agreement with her husband-to-be Debbie finished her drink. 'Have you had a chance to consider my other proposals?' she asked.

'Yes, they are entirely fair, and I agree to them all. Have you chosen an estate agent?' Paul asked.

Debbie looked even more relieved. She had selected the nearest estate agent and they had already been around. They had suggested an asking price of £375,000. Paul was invariably staggered at UK house prices. How could the country sustain this level of expenditure for what is just a roof over a person's head? Sandpiper had cost £2,500, why weren't Norfolk Broads riverbanks covered with boats being lived on? It all seemed so irrational. Maybe we were all just sheep.

Debbie agreed that she would visit the estate agent on Monday and formally request them to sell. Paul said that he would do the same on Tuesday to ensure that the agents were confident that both parties agreed to the sale.

The house the Benfields would initially rent in Gothenburg was furnished. Neither of them wanted much of the furniture here and even less of that in Benfield's flat so it would just be one large Transit van which would transport their stuff to Sweden. Benfield had already agreed to sell his immaculate MGB to a fellow enthusiast for £17,500. He'd bought it for only £10,000 two years earlier. 'Vintage and classic cars are a very good investment,' said Benfield.

Until there's a recession, Paul thought but didn't say out loud. He didn't want anything from the house either. 'If in future I get a flat in the city I'll start furnishing from scratch,' he lied.

Having discussed a few more practicalities the evening came to an end. He'd pick up Ben for a normal access day on Thursday. Debbie walked him to the door, kissed him on the cheek and thanked him once more. He walked back to Sandpiper no nearer an A or B decision, but that point was coming, Thursday's access would be the next to last one.

Early Sunday morning he rowed to Ferry Stores to fill up the water containers. He savoured the calm and quiet of the Yare in the early morning. He would miss these moments dreadfully, the gentle splash and rustle of the water as he rowed, the sheer efficiency of this appealingly low tech means of transporting fifty litres of drinking water. He was at one with the environment here, did he *have* to sail away? And if he did would he ever feel the same about anywhere else? In an attempt to avoid these doubts he spent much of the rest of the day in boat maintenance.

He met Jan in the White Hart at 8 p.m. Over their first pint they opened the Dutch chart folio and Paul ran through the places he had visited, which were much fewer than he'd originally planned. In a quiet voice Jan told him that Sandpiper this next time would retain her working Johnson auxiliary engine but that they would have a large thirty litre fuel tank with which he could only rely on getting ten litres into the engine. A roundabout way of saying that the tank would have a twenty-litre space for ... for what?

Jan shook his head. 'Better you don't know.'

Once again Paul felt a sense of affinity with Jan so, over their second pint, asked him, 'Have we genuinely finished with each other when the second run has been completed?'

Jan laughed. 'Yes, it will be over for both of us. Luck can be pushed too far, and I don't want to end up in prison any more than you do. As with nuclear warheads, it's mutually assured destruction. We can't shop you without giving ourselves away. Nor can you do it to us for the same reason. We all stay silent; we all stay free.'

They supped their drinks in silence for a few minutes then, in a low voice, Jan asked, 'Are you actually thinking of leaving with your son, snatching him?'

Paul hesitated, 'What makes you ask?'

Jan said, 'I put two and two together. Your response when Gunton mentioned it on our first meeting. Your mention of red herrings after talking to Rose Bailey. Your studying of Dutch well beyond that which may be expected of a yachtsman planning a cruise.' He left it for a couple of seconds then added. 'And my knowledge of Dutch overseas territories.'

There was no disguising Paul's surprise. Jan smiled then said, 'OK, I see how it is, but your plans are safe with me. A word of warning though, we Dutch are a rather punctilious lot, in the ABCs or Suriname someone will soon notice that you don't have any official status. By the end of the year your son could be reunited with his mother while you are locked up on remand facing a future trial. And I don't want you attempting some form of plea bargaining which would be a threat to my liberty.'

Stunned, Paul stared at the floor. Christ, this man was sharper than he'd taken him for. Denying that he was thinking of snatching Ben seemed pointless. He looked up at Jan. 'What do you suggest then?'

'Consider somewhere in Europe where they are a bit slapdash with paperwork and where there are hordes of other foreign flagged yachts and tourists. Hiding in plain sight you English call it. Mediterranean Spain, the Greek Ionian or maybe Cyprus, either the Greek or Turkish part. I would choose from them,' Jan answered.

'Does Gunton know any of this?' Paul asked.

'No, I wanted to see you now because he's away for a few days and he doesn't like you. If he's sure you're going to attempt a snatch then he'll try to find a way of fucking up your plans while keeping himself safe. I don't think he's bright enough to successfully do that. The problem is that he doesn't know he's not bright enough so may try it and end up exposing me by accident. Neither you nor I deserve to be brought down by the Guntons of this world. I realised your study of Dutch could be leading the Caribbean or South America and that this was unlikely to be your best move, in my opinion,' he added with a smile.

'Thank you, I've taken all that in and appreciate it.'

'So, the second run starts on?' Jan asked.

'I'm looking to leave the mooring on Friday.'

'OK, let's look through the chart folio for a few minutes while I do the Dutch Minister for Tourism bit then we can shake hands as I wish you a good cruise.'

Walking back to Sandpiper he came to the conclusion that the Mediterranean did have a lot of advantages, no ocean crossing for a start. In fact, if Ben was able to pose as a girl for a few weeks then they may even be able to use the French canals to get to the Med. If anyone asked he could say that he and his son/daughter were having an adventure year in the Med before he/she started school - the child was plenty bright enough to still be ahead when joining the school in year two. If not the canals then they could sail as far as, say, Cadiz on Spain's Atlantic coast where they'd anchor and take stock before deciding on the Mediterranean or the Caribbean. There were people who would give their right arm to have that choice. Or preferably, someone else's right arm.

It was ironic though that he felt more kinship with Jan and the big man he'd had dealings with in Holland than with colleagues he'd known for much longer at college. Once more he asked himself if this was telling him that he should be with boating rather than career/academic people?

Awake at first light on Monday he made two packs of sandwiches, filled three water bottles then packed the day's rations into a rucksack before setting off on foot for the railway station to start his long day's worth of travel on public transport. National Express coach to London Victoria where he changed to the Portsmouth coach. Once there he caught two more local buses to be within walking distance of the marina in Gosport. He phoned the Tamar 24's owner to get directions and said he'd be there in five minutes.

The Tamar had a distinctive stern so Paul recognised her from some berths away. As he approached he saw the boat's name - Ruffy Tuffy. Who in their right mind called a boat that? He imagined having to contact the Coastguard with a Mayday or Pan Pan emergency, the officer receiving the call asking. 'Could you repeat your vessel's name, sir?' 'And the nature of the Ruffy Tuffy's distress, sir?' By this time the rest of the staff in the duty room would be wetting themselves with laughter. The Ruffy Tuffy was in distress - it would be a severe test of the coastguard's professionalism to perform, without giggling, the necessary co-ordination of the boat's rescue. Further thought of future humiliations ended as Paul reached the Tamar's cockpit and offered his hand to her owner who introduced himself as Gil Ryder.

'What made you call her Ruffy Tuffy?' asked Paul, feeling infantile even as he said the name.

'Not me, the original owner named her. I intended to change it but sort of got used to it. It's not one people forget,' replied Ryder.

Unforgettable is absolutely not what I need, Paul thought, before getting down to looking critically at the boat.

Two hours later he had a list of pros and cons. On the plus side was the boat's generally good condition. The standing and running rigging looked OK. She had very good sails and a nice young Beta 20 engine which started readily and ran smoothly. The cockpit felt as safe a place as it could be given that it was the open area between the fore and aft cabins.

On the minus side was the headroom. Paul could not stand upright in either cabin except at one point immediately on entry to the forecabin, and then only with the hatch removed. However, he could stand upright to steer while under the shelter at the forward end of cockpit. The forecabin had a lot crammed into it so as a relaxing place it felt on the small side. The aft cabin was more spacious and would be Ben's if he bought the boat and put Plan A into action. A double minus point was the boat's name which would have to change, not in itself a difficult operation but registering the new name took time he may not have.

Paul told Gil Ryder he was interested but had another two boats to view and he would let him know within a week. It was the standard yachtie get-out in this sort of situation.

Later, on the London Victoria bound coach he closed his eyes and let his mind drift - there was something familiar about the Tamar owner, had he been on TV? Or was he a ClanCo contact from years ago? It wouldn't come. He tried unsuccessfully to doze for the rest of the journey. The coach slowed as it reached south London traffic then suddenly it came.

Gil Ryder! The catchy chorus of a (Caribbean?) pop song from years ago. *Gil an' Golly Rider, Gil an' Golleee.* Probably not the correct words but they were what he heard. How long ago was that? And, with the decisions in front of him at the moment, how could his mind work on something as trivial as probably misheard pop song lyrics? Just another example of displacement activity he supposed, work on something lightweight he could cope with rather than deal with the real problem. And who was it a week or two ago giving Anneke's parents the example of losing your keys in a dark street then going to look for them in a nearby well-lit one? Fiddling while Rome burned, there were plenty of apt sayings. He wasn't pioneering any new sort of behaviour, just taking the easy decoy activity. As the coach inched its way along the last mile into Victoria, he began to see the funny side of the boat's name - *Gil an' Golly Rider, Ruffy Tuffeee*. It occurred to him then that Golly might be a politically incorrect sequence of five letters these days, ah well.

He'd installed the Amazon Kindle e-reader app on the mobile and when the second coach finally shook off London he continued to read Philip Hoare's excellent Rising Tide Falling Star. A short while later, without putting any conscious effort into it, he suddenly knew what he would change the Tamar's name to, if he bought her - Calliope Jack. A few pages ago in the book the author described how in the 1870s the British Navy ship Calliope called at Samoa. British naval ships represented the crown and it was usual for the ship to be given a present. These presents were often animals and the Admiralty had established a Sailor's Zoo on Whale Island in Portsmouth harbour to house these animals. On Samoa, HMS Calliope was given a parrot which was, as customary, enrolled as a member of the crew and named Jack. Shortly after leaving Samoa, Calliope went down in a storm with the loss of all hands except Jack, the only crew member equipped with wings instead of hands. He flew back to Samoa and was some time later presented to the next navy ship to visit. This time he made it to the Sailor's Zoo where he lived for a further 39 years, the zoo's longest living resident. He died in 1919. It couldn't be better for the Tamar, named in memory of a successful escaper who lived a long life in his new environment. And this year was the centenary of Jack's death! Calliope Jack it would be. Thank you, Philip Hoare.

It was well after 10 p.m. when he got back to Sandpiper, tired but successful in that he'd found a boat that would do them, come up with a great name for her and tested the efficiency of Plan A's transport of man and boy to the new boat within the eight hour access day timing. Yes, Plan A would work.

Tuesday and Wednesday were not the most successful of days spent on the internet in the city library, trawling mostly through Wikipedia entries. Although the Dutch speaking islands of Aruba, Bonaire and Curacao looked suitable at first glance - low crime rates, high standard of living, good climate, plenty of yacht harbours - they were such obvious destinations for water gypsies such as himself and Ben that their governments had established plenty of defences such as thirty day visas which were able to be extended only if applicants met certain criteria. Criteria he and Ben would not be able to meet. The only way he could get Ben into a school would be to become a citizen and, since all these islands were affiliated to the Netherlands, this meant (in affect) applying for Dutch citizenship, not an option for fugitives. He realised that this was the first time he'd permitted himself to describe Ben and himself as fugitives. The only way he could meet the criteria for citizenship would be to live in a country long enough to meet and marry a local woman - the great train robber Ronnie Biggs managed to live in Brazil for many years by that route, fathering a son, Paul remembered. Maybe Biggs was right in the sense that the answer was to go to a larger, less well organised South American country, but (back to Wikipedia once more) this often meant a country with a higher crime rate. He re-investigated Suriname on the northeast coast of South America, bordered by Brazil to the south, French Guiana to the east and Guyana to the west. Suriname had been affiliated to the Netherlands in the past but gained independence in 1975. In terms of ethnicity Suriname's population was highly diverse so he and Ben would not stand out as obvious foreigners. Dutch, French and English were three of the many languages spoken and, even better, Sranan

Tongo, an English-based creole language was widely used. By the time he sat back aboard his boat on Wednesday evening it had become clear that if they went for the Atlantic crossing then it would be to Suriname. However, there was no way of avoiding the fact that the list of practical difficulties was growing.

As usual he picked up Ben at 9 a.m. on Thursday. They took the train to Great Yarmouth and spent the morning on the beach. That day Ben's heart didn't seem to be in castle building and as they ate lunch in a cafe Ben said that he wanted to spend the afternoon on Sandpiper.

'You want to remember our times together making things on the boat?' asked Paul.

Ben nodded in reply and put down his knife and fork. Taking the hint Paul left his half-finished plate of fish and chips and they caught the next train back to the village. Aboard Sandpiper Paul let his son choose the activity and found that he had to demonstrate in more depth than before how the behaviour of a structure depends on both its shape and on the material of which it is made. A combination Paul could probably demonstrate better with scissors, glue and Sandpiper's motley collection of makings here than with Ben's Lego Technic at home. 'When you are in Sweden will you make things with cardboard and glue as well as Lego Technic?' he asked.

'Yes, 'member what Daddy showed me,' Ben answered, then looked at his father and burst into tears. Paul cuddled his son, part of him wanting simply to reassure Ben, part of him willing his son to say that he didn't want to go to Sweden, wanted to stay with Daddy, in which case it would be Plan A or Plan A.

In a few minutes Ben was able to speak. 'You always here on Sandpiper?'

It was not what he was hoping to hear but … 'Yes, Daddy and Sandpiper,' Paul replied smiling.

'Mummy said when Ben is older he can fly from Sweden to stay with Daddy here.'

'Daddy will always love you and will always welcome you with open arms wherever Sandpiper and Daddy are,' said Paul, demonstrating the open arms and meaning every word he said while the back of his mind registered the awful fact that Ben had accepted he won't see his father for a long time. From there it followed that he must also have accepted that his stepfather is to be the main man in his life. In fact, Benfield's already the main man, it's himself who's the now-and-again father. Ben spends much more time with Benfield and has adapted to him. Benfield the Stepfather. Benfield the Conqueror. At that moment Paul also realised that the hollow feeling in his stomach was a fact as well as a well-worn cliché.

It was almost 5 p.m. They packed things away and

closed the hatch. Once on the dyke path Ben asked his father to walk on a little way and not watch while he said goodbye to Sandpiper. Paul did as instructed and heard the small boy saying something but could not make out the words. When Paul lifted his son onto the bike seat he asked if Ben was happy with his goodbye. 'Yes, told Sandpiper to look after Daddy when they go sailing.'

He felt tears roll down his cheeks as he hugged his son, 'My lovely Ben,' was all he could manage out loud, his whole being swelling with pride at this small boy's demonstration of love for the father he thought he would not see for a long time.

A quarter of an hour later he apologised to Debbie for being late due to Ben's desire to say goodbye to Sandpiper.

'I'm not surprised, he's very fond of your boat,' laughed Debbie.

'Is it OK if I phone in a few days to make arrangements for what will be my last access day?'

'The last in this country for a while you mean. It won't be the last last will it?'

'Sorry. You're right, I did mean the last here. I'm just not sure which day it will be.'

'No problem, call when you know.' She smiled, a woman sufficiently sure of her future to exude cordiality and reasonableness.

TWELVE

2039:

Ay Markou to Preveza

The alarm shrills at 0540. He dresses quickly and steps out into the cockpit convincing himself that he can just sense the beginnings of the morning wind. Flicking on the engine isolator he moves to the foredeck and starts the process of hauling up a few metres of chain, resting for a couple of minutes then hauling a few metres more. He recalls that his younger self could raise 40 metres of chain in one hauling but in his mid-fifties he's evolved a technique he can cope with and sticks to it. Eventually he stows the anchor neatly, walks back to the cockpit and puts the electric engine into forward, turning the boat and motoring quietly through the other yachts still at anchor. Once clear he raises full sail, switches off the engine and starts tacking slowly across the bay only turning north when they can make in one close reach the passage to a point between the headland and a small island to its north. Progress is slow, the

235

mountains are breathing very lightly this morning and in a couple of hours they start to be overtaken by the motoring yachts of crews who made a more leisurely start to the day. He is not tempted to follow suit, experience of local weather conditions tells him that they'll reach the inner harbour entrance before the light morning wind runs out.

Approaching Preveza from the east in a light north-easterly is always a pleasure, the sun picking out more and more detail of the town's long water frontage, yachts med-moored stern on to the quay, many restaurants and bars behind. A standard Greek scene some would say but he's proud of his adopted home. Finances now dictate that he can never afford to eat out again but, right this minute, he seems to have given up caring. 'Tonight, I will eat out at Helens', he tells Victoria.

Nearing the town, he moves around the boat setting up fenders and ropes to both sides. They don't have a permanent mooring in the inner harbour and so have to be ready to take up any spot which looks suitable.

A last supper he supposes, presenting himself at the restaurant around 8 p.m. On the increasingly rare nights out he has always gone to Helens where she invariably greets him with hugs and kisses, chiding him for not dining there more often, though of course she knows why. She also knows exactly what he will have to eat, it never varies - a small (one skewer) souvlaki, a Greek salad and a 50cl bottle of locally brewed retsina. She shouts his order through to the kitchen and brings him the retsina, a glass and a carafe of tap water. They have a mutual feeling for each other and indulge in another cuddle. Not for the first time he thinks about whether they could have been an item, though this is an academic topic as the occasionally opened kitchen door reveals the fact that husband No 3 is still on the scene and preparing his souvlaki. Perhaps it is simply good to have this level of mutual no-strings-attached attraction. Nothing permanent will come from their feelings for each other but it gives great pleasure to know that someone for whom you have this level of, well ... affection? love? lust? feels the same about you. To this person you are a bit of all right. He laughs to himself, it's an expression his grandfather might have used, why had he thought of it now?

After the meal she brings him an even larger than usual slug of ouzo. This never figures on the bill. He sits, sipping his drink, watching Helen moving through the customers. They are busy, there's a flotilla of sixteen yachties in tonight plus a few of her Greek regulars. She moves provocatively, is this because she knows he's watching or is that unwarranted vanity on his part? She still has a trim waist and generous hips and he remembers, years ago now, seeing her sitting astride her pink scooter, facing away from him - the lovely shape formed by her waist as it curved outward to become her hips in tight jeans. He imagined her sitting on him instead of the scooter - soft, feminine and virtually weightless. Weightless! His imagination had always been superior to his reality. Sitting there now he is not surprised to find that he has the first erection in a long time. It is sustained as she occasionally passes his chair, her hip lightly brushing his shoulder. She knows what she is doing and is enjoying it as much as he. Later, having both returned to his usual flaccid state and finished his drink, he pays the bill of 46 drachma and hugs Helen goodnight.

'When we are quiet you can just sit at a table with a glass of water. Think of it as advertising. With a menu in front of you we will not look so empty. You can finish writing it here. And sometimes we will be alone', she whispers. He thanks her and promises to come back soon then finds he has to turn quickly away as he feels tears forming.

How good Preveza has been to him. In the cool of the evening the waterfront is lively. Elderly Greeks sit at their small barbecues offering grilled corn on the cob. He usually thinks of the corn as scorched rather than grilled but it's a cheap late-night snack and surprisingly tasty. African men spread their wares on the pavement. He is offered a watch for only 200 drachma, Rolex he's assured, they always are. Shaking his head politely he walks slowly on. The ice cream parlour is still doing business, but this is an indulgence he'll avoid. He is lightheaded, happy and emotional. Financial worries will be back again tomorrow, but he seems to be able to put them aside. He is in the moment, this is his place, he is not the complete outsider here.

Nearing the northeast corner of the inner harbour he suffers another episode of what he's previously described as re-positioning. Objects had moved - the area with two cash machines was now ahead on his right and the corner of the inner harbour beside him to the left. This sudden rearrangement of things he was seeing had happened before but this time he's in a place where his memory says there's a low wall to his left, regardless of what his sight indicates. He shuffles slowly and cautiously left until he can feel the wall then sits on it for the short time it takes before his place memory and his current view agree with each other once more. A few minutes ago he'd been happy and confident but now ... now there was a sense of foreboding, a sense of things becoming worse. Previous re-positionings had only occurred when he was extremely tired yet relieved, a few hours after successfully weathering some particularly stressful situation. Sitting on the wall he replayed the last major episode, many years ago but unforgettable.

Bordering the west coast of Italy, the Tyrrhenian Sea is renowned for its fickle winds. It had been nearly three days and nights of frustrating sailing/drifting south between Acciaroli and the Strait of Messina. He'd been on his own and thus sleepless for over sixty hours as they entered the strait around 10 p.m. Here in mythology the sirens Scylla and Charybdis lured ancient sailors to their death. In modern reality it's a place of bizarre whirlpools and eddies and in the dark his tired mind struggled to keep what he thought was a steady course. In this state everything is against you here - night anglers in small unlit boats can't be seen until you're almost on them so you have to be constantly vigilant. Ferries crossing between Sicily and the mainland are the same shape fore and aft so each one has to be stared at to see if it's going to be a hazard. In theory you should be able to tell which way a ship is going by the position and colour of its navigation lights but this is impossible with the various illuminations of a large city like Messina in the background. It would have been disastrous to go into re-positioning mode here but he endured and got the boat safely into Reggio di Calabria's small vessel harbour by 3 a.m., only to be immediately hailed by the duty ormeggiatoro demanding a lengthy form filling performance before he was free to crash out for a few hours. Later that same morning he was walking back to the boat from shopping in town, still wobbly on his sea legs and profoundly tired but also elated at getting to Reggio and now having two bags of fresh fruit and veg. Suddenly his view contained traffic, kerbs and pedestrian crossings but they were nowhere near where they had been a second earlier. He'd stood still closing then opening his eyes hoping to match what had been there before then, in this unfamiliar place, losing confidence in his ability to recall what he thought had been there before. He'd been rescued by an elderly couple who guided him to a seat, soft voices asking if he was OK? He had restaurant Italian at best so couldn't go much beyond 'Grazie mille signor e signora'. After a few minutes he'd asked them (by mime) to show him the pedestrian crossing which, thankfully, proved to be the one he could also see. And so, he got back safely to the boat, later making light of the incident by composing a headline,

Elderly couple help fit young man across road.

It wasn't quite *Man bites dog* but at least it was accurate. Or at least, he looked as if he was fit.

At that time he had the excuse of being pushed to his limits in the Strait of Messina so some reaction was, perhaps, understandable. But what is his excuse now? The interaction with Helen, the worsening finances, Victoria's health? If this is the onset of a more widespread lack of belief in what he is seeing then what is the point of continuing? We are completely reliant on our sense of things growing larger or smaller in a regular way as we move toward or away from them. And that this happens with respect to the relative speed of movement (or non-movement) of ourselves and the objects we see. Take this sense away and we are nowhere, or more accurately, we don't know where we are.

Victoria is waiting in the cockpit and comes to his arms. It's an evening with both his loved females. Neither truly attainable and, somehow, loved the more deeply for it.

THIRTEEN

2019

Back on Sandpiper he reviewed the situation, interrupted by having to field a call from Gunton wanting confirmation that he was leaving the mooring tomorrow to start the second 'run'. Paul confirmed that he would be and ended the call. It was part of the plan; they would leave tomorrow to make it look as if Sandpiper was on her way. He'd stick to his plan of holing up in Lowestoft's inner harbour for his last few days in the UK.

After dinner he walked slowly down the dyke for a last look at the boats which had been Sandpiper's neighbours for the last couple of years. He succumbed to sentimentality, looking with affection at the battered, careworn appearance of most of the boats, their names a mixture of puns (Nautigal) or old sitcom references ('Er Indoors) or mother-in-law jibes (Tell 'im Janet) or, on what was probably the scruffiest Davison's Dyke boat, a jokey regret (Never Again 2). He had been comfortable here. It was a place he would miss.

He thought back to his 'simple' life of a few weeks ago. Simple in the sense that he had been completely unaware of other people's moves which were to impinge on him.

Friday morning and an hour into the ebb he tied the dinghy onto the foredeck and cast off. Sentimentality had not completely evaporated, they motored slowly down the dyke, Paul issuing silent goodbyes to his old floating friends. There was a light wind from the west, so he raised full sail and moved slowly downriver, taking his last look at familiar village surroundings. He caught a glimpse of Jenny through the open door of the Ferry Stores and a few minutes later viewed the stern of Gunton's boat (Candy Girl) without seeing the owner. Slowly on past the Mermaid Cove Marina, as usual all gleaming white fibreglass and shining stainless steel in the late August sun. The enemy, he will miss even them. Rose had been gone five or six weeks now and another gin palace lay in Audacity's old mooring. He caught a brief glimpse of Jan's boat at the far end of the marina before trees blocked their view.

On they sailed, more quickly now as trees gave way to grazing marshes and the tidal stream grew stronger. He even managed a spot of affection for the tall chimneys of the Cantley sugar factory. At Reedham he tied Sandpiper to the bridge's waiting pontoon and phoned Oulton Broad Yacht Station to book a lock and associated bridges opening for 10.30 a.m. the following day. Through the swing bridge when it opened he steered into the New Cut and at its far end tied Sandpiper up once more to hassle her mast down to get under the fixed bridge at Haddiscoe. He left the mast down and motored on the few remaining miles to anchor at the western end of Oulton Broad for the night. He used the boat's block and tackle to raise the mast, a difficult job with the dinghy occupying most of the foredeck. The last time he was here he'd received his criminal payout, of which he'd spent very little so far. That evening he simmered vegetables in one pan and boiled a kettle for couscous. He topped the final plateful with grated cheese and sat eating his supper in the cockpit, facing the setting sun. It seemed a long time ago that he and Anneke sat at anchor off the Marken lighthouse. He found tears rolling down his cheeks once more. The decision, Plan A or Plan B, had to be made this weekend.

Bridge and lock openings went without hitch on Saturday and they were through into Lowestoft's inner harbour by 10.45 a.m. He'd put no effort into finding a mooring for a week (perhaps two) so decided to motor around looking for a vacant inner berth which was not immediately obvious to anyone coming by road. Having found one he'd ask if it were available for up to 14 days. It was clearly his lucky day as he found one at the first boatyard south of the bridge and agreed a two-week berth for £80. Sandpiper was secure on her new and paid for mooring by 11.30 a.m. Things had gone so well that he decided to treat himself to a carvery lunch at the Wherry Hotel which he enjoyed while watching what seemed to be an all-comers dinghy race on Oulton Broad. Yet more Broads scenes he would miss.

A or B? He forced himself to sit on his boat for the rest of the day and into the evening ...

Plan A. Assuming he bought the Tamar 24 in Gosport he'd have to go down the day before snatch day (he abbreviated this to SD-1 in his notes) and stock the boat with enough food to cover their projected passage to wherever - it looked likely to be Cadiz from where they could head east into the Mediterranean or south for the Canaries to await the best time for an Atlantic crossing to Suriname. He'd also have to buy a lot of clothing (boy and girl) for Ben and had been making note of sizes on his son's clothes labels when the opportunity occurred. This was a great deal of travelling and shopping on SD-1 to be followed on SD by another Lowestoft to village to Gosport journey with Ben, doubtless a tension rich journey from which he'd be seriously tired. He'd have to get some sleep on SD night so decided that they would set off at first light on SD+1. The passage plan was straightforward. Head south to mid channel then west into the Atlantic then south once more when he felt that they could make Cadiz without tacking. There was no way of registering in time a new name for the Tamar before they left so they'd have to suffer the infantile one until they found somewhere they could safely stay (and receive mail) for the two weeks or so it would take before they had a registration document in the name of Calliope Jack. There were other factors. To minimise the risk of being seen by Gunton and Jan he would have to avoid being in the village other than on access day (aka SD). He must have another overnight visit to his mother, say on SD-4 and SD-3. So, if snatch day were on Thursday he'd go to his mother tomorrow and return on Monday evening. Keep Tuesday (SD-2) free for any emergency action. Head off early on Wednesday (SD-1) for Gosport and return as early as possible that day for a last night on Sandpiper. On Thursday (SD) he'd say goodbye to his faithful boat and home, ride his bike to the station and catch the train to the village. Pick up Ben as usual but this time catch the train to the city, cycle to the bus station, say a silent goodbye and thank you to the bike and board the coach to London Victoria. They'd arrive at the Tamar in the early evening and cast off at first light on Friday (SD+1). A tight plan but an achievable one. He'd do more research on destinations later, when the opportunity presented itself.

Plan B required much less action. He'd give up Ben without a fight and be as helpful to the family Benfield as he could be during their last few days in the UK. He'd make sure Ben saw no resentment in his father's attitude to their leaving. He'd have a last couple of days with his mother, making a full confession of what he'd done and what he had been considering doing. Then he'd sail off in Sandpiper heading south for wherever.

Late in the evening he reviewed destinations. Jan had been in favour of Spain, Greece or Cyprus, all three of them countries he could access via the French canal system. If it happened at all, Brexit was due to happen at the end of October so there would be no formalities required on entering another EC country before then. The canal route to the Mediterranean was feasible but only if they were not recognised as the man and snatched boy mentioned in some news report. How much publicity would the snatch generate? He recalled that case of the fourteen-year-old schoolgirl who'd eloped with one of her teachers. His memory told him that they were soon caught in France. He could think of no way of finding out how many snatches there had been compared with how many had been publicised. Plan A via the French canals was tempting in that they could do it on Sandpiper, leaving them £5000 better off. And if Ben was able to pose as a girl for the six to eight weeks it would take to reach the Med via the canals, then the risk of detection would be as low as it could be. He decided to sleep on it.

He awoke on Sunday knowing he could not go through with Plan A. Ben had a much better chance of living a fulfilled life with Benfield and Debbie than he did with his father. And certainly a safer one - he thought back to those saw teeth he'd 'seen' outside Ijmuiden harbour and the mythical 'horse on the shore' all those years ago in Fiji. These episodes were not the only ones, when tired and under extreme stress he was not reliable enough to be responsible for a small child. Plan A had originated when he thought that Ben would be with Debbie and having to go to the village school. That situation had changed for the better and he'd seen enough of Benfield to know that the man was genuine - his first question at the end of the Volvo interview had been about Ben's education. And in Gothenburg Ben would be far enough away from any Gunton and Jan retribution. Plan B was the right move, himself the only loser. For him the necessary mindset was one which balanced the loss of his contact with Ben against the gain in his son's welfare. Ben was four years old with everything before him. Ben came first.

The rest of the morning he let his mind drift over options for his own life from now. Once more he treated himself to a carvery lunch and watched dinghy racing on the broad. There were attractions in staying here but without Ben and without Anneke it would be less of a life than it might have been. No, he was going to give in to his desire to play the wanderer. Before Brexit happened, he and Sandpiper would sail off for the Med via the French canals.

In early evening he phoned the Tamar's owner, Gil Ryder, and told a white lie, saying he'd found another boat and would therefore not be pursuing his interest in the Ruffy Tuffy. Ryder was obviously disappointed but understood. Next he phoned his mother and arranged to see her on Wednesday and Thursday. Finally, he phoned Debbie and said that he had decided to sail to the Med and spend some years visiting other countries. He also said that he would forgo his share of the money from the house sale and pass it to her to hold in trust for Ben, and would she please instruct her solicitor to draw up, asap, whatever sort of statement which made Paul's decision legal. Paul added that he would call in to her solicitor's office on Friday to sign the document.

'That is extremely generous, are you sure? How will you manage for money? What about your college career?' Debbie asked.

Paul replied, 'I've thought hard about it. I'll continue to live economically. There's nothing to keep me here now that I know Ben will be well looked after. Can I visit the house for a short time with Ben on Tuesday?'

'Yes of course. We are in a mess with packing, but you will be welcome.'

He slept for over ten hours and awoke on Monday morning feeling relaxed for the first time in some days. It was refreshing not to have to tell lies and not to have plans which must be hidden.

He emailed his notice to the college, apologising for its shortness due to circumstances that he had been unable to control. It was more than a little unsatisfactory but would have to do.

On the French canals it was over 1200 kilometres (over 600 sea miles) from Calais in the north to Port St Louis in the south, all to be done under engine. It would be necessary to replace the little Johnson outboard (who's doppelgänger transported whatever it was across the North Sea) with a younger more powerful engine with which to back up Sandpiper's main one. An internet search ordered on nearest first revealed that the local chandlers had a choice of three which may be suitable. In late morning he walked to the chandlers. A five-year-old Yamaha 8hp with high thrust propeller was the standout engine. He negotiated a price of £1000 to include delivery that day plus the Johnson in part exchange. Late in the afternoon both Sandpiper's main and her new auxiliary engines were running well and ready for the hard work ahead.

It was Tuesday and for the foreseeable future it would be the final time with his son. Ben opened the door.

'Daddy,' he shouted and hugged his father's legs as usual. Paul kissed the top of his son's head before Ben continued, 'Mummy said Sandpiper and you go sailing long way.'

Paul had anticipated this one, 'Yes, you told Sandpiper to look after me so I can safely go sailing all over the Mediterranean now. When you are a little older, I'm sure Mummy and Scott will let you have an email account so we can send each other messages and photographs. You will be able to tell me how you are getting on at school and I will be able to tell you where we are and what we have seen.' Never underestimate the love of a boy for his teddy bear he remembered, so added. 'Oh, and I would also like to know how James is getting on.'

'Yes Daddy. James going to Sweden with me. Come and help Ben pack.'

Two hours went by swiftly and, as he was having tea and cake with the three of them, he realised it was time to go. Shaking Benfield's hand and kissing Debbie on both cheeks he reminded her that he'd call in to the solicitor's office on Friday.

Ben accompanied him to the door. Paul kneeled

down and looked at his son, that slightly long face and curly black hair. The image he would always carry. 'When you are a young man, we will see each other again. Before then we can email each other. You will have a good life with Mummy and Scott. And Daddy will always love you, little one.' Tears flowed unchecked down Paul's face as he kissed his son's forehead. Ben's face was wet with tears also and he was trying to say some words, but they wouldn't form properly. Paul realised that Ben was trying to say something similar to him.

'Thank you, my lovely boy. Go and be with Mummy and Scott now, I'll close the door.' After a small hesitation Ben turned and walked back to the lounge. His father's final view was of his son's small retreating form. Paul closed the door and walked away not daring to look back.

Late morning Wednesday and Paul sat with his mother in her flat enjoying a cup of real coffee. Freshly ground dark beans, brewed in cone and filter paper, it was one of her few indulgences She looked at her son and raised an eyebrow.

'Yes, it tastes as good as ever, what beans are you using?' he asked.

'A fifty-fifty mix of Italian and Javanese,' she replied then, after a short pause added, 'Something has changed, you don't seem as tense as you were on your last visit.'

He looked at his mother, the only person who had loved and cared for him all his life. The person to whom he owed everything. How much should he say? The silence lengthened until his mother spoke again. 'Tell me everything, however awful it is,' she said quietly.

His full confession cascaded out and became incoherent at times, at which point she asked questions. 'So here I sit, the criminal son confessing all to his mother,' he said finally.

She walked across the room to Paul's chair and silently hugged him, his head uncomfortable between her breast and shoulder, his mind knowing that this love and care was what he needed at that moment.

After what seemed a long time she returned to her chair and said, 'Let me attempt a summary, correct me when I'm wrong. You have been living a rather isolated life on your boat in an out of the way dyke. A little removed from the real world, your major focus being the four access hours with Ben on Thursdays. The simplicity of this life was shattered by a terrible few days when your access to Ben was threatened by Debbie, a class disintegrated badly due to your lack of awareness of what the students needed at that time. Thus, your job was under threat, and two criminals had noted your vulnerability and were using the tactic of both tempting you with money and threatening Ben if you didn't take up their offer, the classic carrot and stick. You changed your behaviour to lessen the effect of the first two threats but succumbed to the vulnerability sensed by the criminals. If you could get enough money from them you realised that you could snatch Ben and go. You started planning for this and, while doing so and having been set ticking by Emma, you met Anneke and fell for her. You sailed to Holland and did your first criminal ...' she searched for a suitable word then continued, 'transport job and got paid for it. Anneke chose to stay with the other man she loved then came the final and most devastating of the five bombshells to hit you. Ben, his mother and his soon-to-be-stepfather were moving to Sweden. You made frantic plans for a last-minute snatch then came to your senses. Benfield, you decided, is an entirely suitable stepfather and Ben will be going to an entirely suitable school. You have decided to sail off and live the life of a wanderer on your boat in the Med.' She looked at him with a slight smile then added. 'And leave your poor mother alone here.'

'That's an amazing summary. I see a late career for you as a detective. More seriously though, Gunton and Jan haven't finished with me. They think their second run has started and all my senses say that, even if I did that successfully, there would be more demands. I'd eventually be caught and jailed or end up accidentally drowned.'

'What did Sandpiper transport?' she asked.

Paul noticed that she'd used the words Sandpiper transport rather than you transport and loved her all the more for her protective instinct. 'At first I thought it must be drugs but later realised that neither Gunton nor Jan showed signs of being into drugs. Amsterdam is also a centre for diamonds, and I wondered If we had run high value diamonds, possibly ones smuggled out of the mines by workers.'

'Well, I suppose that's a more socially acceptable crime, if any crime is ever socially acceptable. But you would still end up in prison if caught.'

'I know.'

'And I know that heading off in your own boat is the only real option for the moment. But I so wish it was not. Because Debbie and I don't get on I've accepted that I won't see Ben again or, at best, not see him for a long time. And now the situation is similar for my son.' Her voice broke and Paul hurried across the room, dropped to his knees and pulled his mother to him. On his previous visit she'd known something was amiss with him but what he'd just told her must be a terrible shock.

He kissed her hair and murmured, 'I'm so sorry, Mum, at one point recently I thought I might be able to find a way of being with the three people I loved, yourself, Ben and Anneke but circumstances have taken two of them away ...'

She pushed him gently away. 'From your description of Anneke I would have liked the four of us to live together also.'

Still on his knees in front of her Paul nodded agreement. She continued. 'We have to learn to live with our regrets. Put them aside for long periods to get on with the rest of our lives. Occasionally we succumb to our regrets when the need to do so becomes overwhelming. Then put them aside once more to continue doing whatever it is that we want to do.'

'Yes, and thank you for everything, Mum.'

'It is how I will deal with the absence of my son and his son. Now I am going to make a dramatic gesture, one a scriptwriter would hesitate to put onto the page for fear of appearing over the top.'

Puzzled, he stood up and moved aside. His mother went to the chest of drawers, pulled out the top one completely and dumped its contents (it looked like her underwear drawer) onto her bed. She pointed to the jumbled heap and said. 'I'll redistribute this lot into other drawers.' Sliding the drawer back into its normal place she said. 'Whatever happens there is always a place for you here with me. I'm going to buy you a set of clothes and place them here in what will always be your drawer. Whatever state you get back to me in there will always be a bath, a change of clothes and unconditional love.'

They moved together and hugged tightly. Paul

tried to speak but could manage only a croaky whisper. 'My one solid base in the world is here with you. It always will be, and I am totally grateful for your dramatic gesture.'

'It's time I made you a very late lunch while we discuss how best to spend these last few hours together. I mean the last for some time of course,' she corrected herself.

'We could go to the cinema if there's anything interesting showing. We could view and discuss some of your DVDs here. I could go down the completely wrong road again when discussing Kate Bush lyrics. You could tell me a little more about my father.' He realised that this may not be what she wanted so added, jokingly, 'or we could go clubbin'.'

'Clubbin' with one's son is sooo yesterday. I'm happy with anything else you mentioned though.'

His mother had always been sparing with details about his father and he used to think that he may have been the result of a one-night stand, or worse, his mother didn't know which of her men had fathered him. That was the basis of Mamma Mia with Meryl Streep, he vaguely remembered. 'Tell me more about Dad,' he said.

'It was a whirlwind romance. We met and married quickly and lived in a rented ground floor flat in north London, Kilburn. He was born in Ireland, in the

Limerick area, County Kerry, and brought here as a child when his father got a job with the BBC in Shepherds Bush. Your father was a very good diver, Tom Daley type, not aqualung. Good enough to be part of a team of divers taking part in ceremonies to open newly built or refurbished swimming pools. He was slightly shorter than you with a typical Irish appearance, dark hair, blue eyes, fair complexion. He swept me off my feet at the time we met but it was a very short romance, he died of tuberculosis six weeks before you were born and I fled back to my parents' house for your birth. Until I remarried, you thought my parents were your parents. And they were certainly good parents to you. During this period, I also lost touch with his family.'

'So, my father was an Irishman with a Welsh surname, I'm a mongrel,' he said jokingly.

'Go far enough back and we're all mongrels.'

'Am I like him?'

'A little perhaps, he showed what might be called mild Asperger behaviour these days. His obsession with his diving the main example.'

'So, if he had lived and you'd gone in for the practice of naming your child after the place where he or she had been conceived, I would have been Kilburn Williams.'

She laughed. 'Just be grateful we didn't go in for that practice when living in Sidcup.'

As he laid the table, he thought Kilburn Williams now, a name for an actor, or perhaps a career criminal? No, that was too close to the bone. It also dawned on him that, as he was qualified to apply for Irish citizenship, this may have been useful if Plan A was go. But it was irrelevant now.

It was coming up 4 p.m. when he had the sudden urge to see where his parents had been living and, if his father had not died so early, the place he could call his first home. They took the tube and a short time later walked into Brondesbury Villas. They stood outside the number that had been theirs, or the ground floor of it anyway. 'This is more upmarket than I expected,' he said in surprise.

'Thank you for that! Though the reality is that the area has become much gentrified since our day.'

'I'm sorry, is it hurtful to be here now?'

'No, the opposite. To be here with you at this moment completes some sort of circuit. I can't explain why this is so, but the result is satisfying. I should be thanking you for bringing me here. Now I don't want to share you with the rest of London any more than I have to. If you're happy with this then we'll stay in the flat and be with each other until you go tomorrow. In other words, I'm going to mother you for another twenty-four hours.'

'This is a man ripe for mothering.'

Back at the flat they decided to watch The Mercy together before discussing the film over a light supper. Later, having finished her cheese on toast, she went into challenging mode asking, 'Did you notice anything odd about this film compared with the other two about the Crowhurst story?'

'The casting of the Hallworth and Best characters jarred a little. It's almost as if they hired two actors who looked similar to the real people they were to play then swapped them over for some reason. Do you know why?'

'No I don't, but noticed it as you did. I suppose it's conceivable the actors were hired to play the parts that they did and the similarity to the other one's real life character is entirely accidental. We'll probably never know.'

'They did make a good job of reproducing the Teignmouth Electron though,' Paul said.

'Bigger stars, bigger budget than the film Nic Roeg was associated with, where the more modern trimaran was probably a borrowed one. What about Rachel Weisz's speech at the door of her home?'

'With the pack of hounds at the gate. You were absolutely right, it's completely relevant to today. The scriptwriter and director deserve a medal.'

Thursday's weather was lovely, the sun shining in a

clear blue sky. Changing their minds about staying in the flat they went for a walk in Holland Park and later had a salad lunch in a side street bistro. 'So, this afternoon's film to watch and discuss is ...?' she asked.

'I can't remember the name of the film but it's a Nicholas Roeg one. It's a hypothetical interaction between four public figures in 1950s/60s USA. Marilyn Monroe, Joe DiMaggio, Albert Einstein and Senator Joe McCarthy. I remember that DiMaggio is played by Gary Busey.'

'Insignificance. The other three main actors were Theresa Russell, Tony Curtis and Michael Emil. What makes you choose this one?'

'I remember Marilyn Monroe tells Albert Einstein about playing a role.'

His mother raised her eyebrows, what made her son remember that? 'OK, Insignificance it is.'

Paul had forgotten how old the film was, 1980s. And also how good it was, insignificance shown in many ways - DiMaggio at the end of his career as a baseball star buying packets of chewing gum to see if he was still a player depicted on the packet's give-away collectable card. And the particular bit he'd remembered - Einstein complimenting Monroe on her grasp of relativity and she explaining that she did not know the subject at all but was just playing the role of someone who did, and she had learned her lines well. 'I have wondered if playing the role of father is any more than playing a role as described by the Marilyn Monroe character,' Paul said.

So, that's why he chose this film. His mother took a moment to consider this then said, 'A conventional response to that would have me shocked.' She put her hands in the air in theatrical shock and continued. 'And I would have to answer something like ... of course it's not role playing, there's a bond between father and child beyond the playing of any role.' She put her hands down. 'And a cop-out response would have me saying I don't know, I'm a mother not a father.'

Paul smiled at the last part. 'I don't want to diminish fatherhood but there are many examples of men being good stepfathers. Men with no direct DNA connection providing the necessary love, care, protection and guidance to fulfil the role of father. I accept that it's different for a mother and child. You grew me. I am part of you and always will be.'

'There are many examples of good stepmothers too,' she said. 'And I do understand what you mean when you say playing the father role. And I am heartened by the detachment you've just shown, it is one method of dealing with your regrets.'

'In what way?' he asked.

'Have you seen the film Shadowlands? Anthony Hopkins and Debra Winger?'

'I don't recall it.'

'The film was based on C S Lewis' book Surprised by Joy. In the book the author demonstrates that one cannot both contemplate and enjoy at the same time. He gives an example of looking at an attractive young woman and realising that it is not possible to contemplate the nature of lust and be at the same time lustful. You have contemplated the nature of fatherhood and in doing so diminished the worst of your pining for Ben. The ability to step sideways and consider the nature of things, contemplate to use Lewis' word, is a valuable asset.'

'My wise old mother,' he said affectionately.

'Your wise what mother?'

'My beautiful wise mother.'

'Well, the last word's accurate,' she laughed.

He knew that now was the time to go so continued the light tone by saying. 'At this point the son tells his beautiful and wise mother that he is leaving before he becomes sufficiently weepy and clingy to make her ashamed of him.'

His mother smiled, nodded agreement, moved over to the chest of drawers and pointed at what was now his part of it.

'Yes Mum, my one solid point in the world is here.'

At the door they hugged each other for a long time before she gently pushed him away, 'Take care, my Paul, and keep in contact.'

He promised to do so and left. At the corner he

paused and looked back. She was still there, outside her door. They waved then he walked around the corner and out of sight, realising as he did so that his mother had just received the same receding view of her son as he had of Ben two days ago. On the train back to Lowestoft he acknowledged how lucky he had been to have such an intelligent and thoughtful mother and also a son who gave every sign of matching her. A pity about the generation between he thought ruefully, in this case the best genes skipped a generation. At Colchester he looked at the station clock, 7 p.m. In forty hours, Sandpiper and her flawed owner would be on passage for Calais and their new life.

Friday was busy. He caught a train to the city and signed the statement assigning his share of the house to Debbie to hold in trust for Ben. Back in Lowestoft by late morning he spent the rest of the day shopping for provisions and for petrol, buying four extra fuel cans to give Sandpiper a capacity of nearly sixty litres. Finally, he tied the bike on top of the dinghy. It was very crowded and, doubtless, dangerous on the foredeck now but there was little choice. The bike was a necessity, there would be places on the French inland waterways where he would have to go some distance for petrol, cans strapped to the bike.

He was up early on Saturday. At 8 a.m. he phoned the

bridge and booked Sandpiper onto the list for the 10 a.m. opening. In the outer harbour by 10:15 he raised full sail in a good northwest to west wind and set off for Calais, twenty-four to thirty hours sailing away. The wind was due to back to the southwest later so they pressed on, hoping to be off North Foreland by the time the wind backed that far. Off North Foreland they'd turn east for Calais, concentrating on their crossing of the world's busiest shipping lane. For now though they headed south becoming further from the Suffolk coast as they did so. At one point he could just see as a tiny column in the distance his old friend the Orfordness lighthouse. He shouted what must now be a final goodbye and expressed, out loud, his regret that he would no longer sail these waters which had, over the years, given such pleasure and, yes, occasional pain. It was sentimental behaviour, he knew, but couldn't give a damn.

They sailed on through the rest of the day and night being far enough from the coast for Suffolk and Essex to vanish below the western horizon. England would not return until they could see the Kent coast. The wind backed as forecast in the morning and they were close hauled in lumpy seas off North Foreland for a while. Eventually they were able to bear away for Calais and Sandpiper's motion became easier as they broad reached towards the French coast. Paul kept looking back watching his home country recede, as he had watched son go, he realised. His last view of England was a tiny smudge of Kent on the horizon. It was not there when he looked again.

He thought how, on this last stretch across the channel to Calais, they would cross the track of the beautiful clipper Audacity which, five or six weeks ago now, carried Rose and her crew south then west from here. If she had invited him to help her now, he would jump at the chance. It was another example of bad timing - during lesson one at the great University of Life you learn that opportunities occur when you are least able to take advantage of them and threats occur when you are least able to deal with them. Clearly he'd been taking his practicals this summer. Did he get a pass? Well, he still lived, if that was regarded as a pass.

They picked up a waiting buoy outside Calais' yacht basin around 2 p.m. on Sunday. He was feeling a little shaken but pleased with himself at having arrived safely. He settled down with a mug of tea in the cockpit. It would be an hour or so before the water level rose enough for the gate into the yacht basin to open and his thoughts strayed back to the events of the summer. He'd responded to the opportunities and threats as seemed appropriate at the time. Had the timing of them been different then his responses would have differed also. It could therefore be argued that it was nothing more than chance that he'd arrived in this place at this time. The net result was that on the way to this point in his life he'd lost Emma, Anneke and Ben. The loss of Ben had been his own choice based on what he thought best for his son. Emma and Anneke had chosen a career and another man respectively. This was as well perhaps, and both of the partings of the ways had been kind and loving ones. And his mother? From the outside her gesture in allocating him that drawer might appear trivial but he was the one person who knew what it had cost this most independent of women. He also knew that the love conveyed by her gesture would sustain him.

He glanced at the clock in the cabin, almost time for the gate to open. Over the next couple of days, he would lower and secure the mast and generally prepare Sandpiper for her 760-statute mile journey to the Mediterranean, passing through 230 locks and 5 tunnels. Doubtless he would be a tired man by the time they entered the Med through the final lock at Port St Louis du Rhone. From that point he would live at the slow and economical pace of the wanderer. A simple life. This time it would stay that way.

FOURTEEN

2039:

Preveza to Ormos Rougas

In Preveza's inner harbour he lowers their yacht's mast and stows it securely along the coach roof as if preparing for a winter ashore. He ties rope from the two ends of the mast to the deck to minimise the chance of snagging fishing equipment. From time to time, passing boat people comment that there is plenty of sailing left this year to which he replies that he has to go away for a while. His I'm-too-busy-to-interrupt attitude is such that nobody ventures a follow up comment.

While it is still light, he fixes a torch to the inside of the cabin roof and places a screwdriver where it can be easily reached. He uses a portable vice to crush and thus disable the position transmitter which became compulsory for pleasure craft a few years ago. It is an enjoyable act of destruction.

Victoria is old, it is amazing she has lasted so long.

It is said that only humans are aware that they will die at some point but lately he has begun to think that she is hanging on because she is worried about how he will cope with her death. This evening she sits on his lap as they look at each other. Tears roll down his cheeks as she manages a short burst of purring, the first in many months. She knows. This wise cat. This beautiful grey tabby.

The south-easterly has not yet arrived but it's on its way, the resulting cloud cover ensuring that it is a dark night. At 2 a.m. he takes two lengths of rope, a box of small hardware items and his toolbag over to the useful-bits-help-yourself area in the ablution block. It's a return gesture in thanks for all those free bits that have kept his boat going over the years. At 2:30 a.m. he casts off and, showing no lights, they motor quietly east down the gulf. Most of the boat's battery power has been expended by the time they enter the wide bay of Ormos Rougas. He watches the depth sounder and selects a position in the deepest water, just before the shallows which reach some distance from the shore. There is neither wind nor swell so they will stay in this position. He moves forward and flakes the anchor and all its chain over the forehatch making it impossible to open from the inside. Victoria is in the cabin and he joins her, locking the door from the inside. He fully opens the vent over the cooker then pushes the cabin key through, hearing it bounce off the deck followed by a splash as it enters the water. Victoria watches as he unscrews the galley sink outlet hose. It is below the waterline and Ormos Rougas spurts quietly in as he pulls off the hose.

He stands feet apart for stability, thanking his boat for its faithful service, thanking Victoria for her love and friendship. Together the three of them are a unit. They have run their course. He picks Victoria up, putting her front paws over his shoulder. She looks at him then closes her eyes. Tears roll down his cheeks once more as water gradually replaces air. It is up to the cabin table now and pages of the unpublished novel start to float free. A blurry page comes into view, *molecule* he reads and smiles, remembering his poor explanation of water and air, the two mediums we and the things we make move in. But only one of which we can breathe he hears himself say.

His mother died three years ago. On the internet he's found that his estranged son has finished his PhD and is heading for an academic career. No one will mourn. No one will know. Victoria is 16 and weak with mouth cancer. She can barely eat now. Their yacht is over 70 years old and in need of major expenditure. Her repair patches have repair patches. He has only two frugal months of money left. None of them can go on. The boat, the man, the cat and the novel will die here, and the world will not be one iota the poorer. He recalls the android, at the end, telling the blade runner, *all these things will be lost in time*, *like tears in rain.* And tears in a sinking.

And Helen? She is astute, she saw his tears forming as he turned to go that last night at her restaurant. She knows he is unlikely to return but will, perhaps, think of him from time to time, as may his son as he gets older. Some people will also remember Victoria and their boat. For some years we live on in the minds of those who knew us and when they go, so do we. Few of us will ever gain a Wikipedia entry or earn a place in a history book, if history books themselves have a long-term future.

He realises Victoria has gone. Her head will soon be engulfed. He kisses her for the final time and holds her tight with his right hand. His left hand is touching the cabin roof, the man the conduit between cat and boat. He remains steady in this ultimate test of self-will. At the end his mind flickers from memory to memory. His mother comforting him as a child. A snatch of Sylvia Plath's poem Edge, *we have come so far.* A small boy with a gap-toothed smile saying *strong bond stone.* Ormos Rougas accepts them, soon its surface is still.

ABOUT THE AUTHOR

He lives in Norfolk with his partner. He has worked as an engineer, a college lecturer and an occasional writer for the UK's biggest selling boating magazine. Single handedly he sailed an elderly catamaran around the world, 1991 to 1993. The collected newsletters from the circumnavigation are available as an Amazon Kindle eBook - The Journal of the Alleda. jpcorridan@gmail.com

Printed in Great Britain
by Amazon

46775749R00160